FORBIDDEN TRAIL . . .

It was obvious that Crystal Dickens had been there, had lit a fire, drank some coffee, and opened a can of beans. The signs were all there to be read.

And they'd been seen and interpreted by eyes other than those of the half-breed. Three riders who had been heading down the trail from the northwest. Heavily built by the looks of it. They had come upon the campsite after the woman left, and had followed her.

Edge had a good idea who the three riders were. Bad company. Crystal didn't stand a chance against them. Edge would have only the element of surprise on his side.

Edge paused at the campsite only a moment. Then he took the same route. . . .

WALK ALONG THE BRINK OF FURY:

THE EDGE SERIES

Westerns By GEORGE G. GILMAN

#20: SULLIVAN'S LAW	(361-7, $3.50/$4.50)
#21: RHAPSODY IN RED	(426-5, $3.50/$4.50)
#22: SLAUGHTER ROAD	(427-3, $3.50/$4.50)
#23: ECHOES OF WAR	(428-1, $3.50/$4.50)
#24: SLAUGHTERDAY	(429-X, $3.50/$4.50)
#25: VIOLENCE TRAIL	(430-3, $3.50/$4.50)
#26: SAVAGE DAWN	(431-1, $3.50/$4.50)
#27: DEATH DRIVE	(515-6, $3.50/$4.50)
#28: EDGE OF EVIL	(526-1, $3.50/$4.50)
#29: THE LIVING, THE DYING AND THE DEAD	(531-8, $3.50/$4.50)
#30: TOWERING NIGHTMARE	(534-2, $3.50/$4.50)
#31: THE GUILTY ONES	(535-0, $3.50/$4.50)
#32: THE FRIGHTENED GUN	(536-9, $3.50/$4.50)
#33: RED FURY	(562-8, $3.50/$4.50)
#34: A RIDE IN THE SUN	(571-7, $3.50/$4.50)

#37

EDGE

VENGEANCE AT VENTURA

BY

George G. Gilman

PINNACLE BOOKS
WINDSOR PUBLISHING CORP.

PINNACLE BOOKS

are published by

Windsor Publishing Corp.
475 Park Avenue South
New York, NY 10016

Third printing: February, 1992

Printed in the United States of America

For:
R. W.
who threw a party out west—
not of the necktie variety.

VENGEANCE
AT VENTURA

Chapter One

THE San Juan River in the south eastern corner of Utah was little more than a trickle of water along a shallow muddy trench when Edge and Crystal Dickens halted their horses and the animals dipped their heads to drink.

"It seems to me," the woman growled sourly, "that we have ridden an awfully long way to get precisely nowhere."

She took off her sweat-stained white Stetson, made a token attempt to finger comb her hair, then grimaced at its greasy feel and replaced the hat.

"Everywhere is somewhere, lady," the man answered, face impassive as he arced the butt of a cigarette into the dust-clouded water and heard the glowing tobacco hiss.

She swung to left and right in her saddle, surveying the desolate terrain of rock and sand and dried up brush and cactus vegetation spread out on all sides. And her grimace hardened into a scowl.

"So where is this?"

"Figure we're close to a place that's like nowhere else in this whole country," Edge answered evenly.

She vented a hollow laugh. "You could've fooled me. This piece of real estate doesn't look much different from every other mile of country we've covered since we left Irving."

Her eyes directed a weary challenge toward him.

Edge pointed a finger to the northeast, then the northwest. "There's Colorado and there's Utah." Then he stabbed a crooked thumb over his right shoulder and his left. "New Mexico. Arizona. Ain't no place else where four states or territories corner like this."

Anger flared across her face and her voice was shrill. "Shit, Edge, we've come all these miles for you to give me a geography lesson?"

The man raised a hand to rasp a thumb over the bristles on the side of his jaw, apparently unmoved by the ill-tempered outburst. But then his arm swung toward her. Very fast. She started a gasp of alarm, but this was curtailed by a squeal of pain as the back of his hand hit her cheek. She had withdrawn her feet from the stirrups and now released the reins to grab for the saddlehorn. But the fingerhold she got was not enough and she was knocked off the horse. The squeal lengthened and became a scream of greater pain when she slammed against the sun-baked mud of the river bed.

The scream ended and she sobbed, looking up at Edge from between the legs and under the belly of her still drinking stallion. "You sonofabitch!" she rasped through clenched teeth. "That is the last time you beat up on me!" She sobbed again and climbed unsteadily to her feet, to glare

2

at him hatefully across the saddle. "We're through! Like we should have been back in Irving! I should have known you were lying when you told me you didn't enjoy hurting women! A man like you!"

The man called Edge nodded and touched the brim of his hat with his fingernails. "No sweat, lady. First time I hit you was because you acted like a whore. This time because you talked dirty like one. Been nice knowing you. Some of the other times."

He tugged on the reins to raise his gelding's head then heeled the animal forward, through the three-feet-wide stream and up the slope of the hard packed and myriad cracked bed on the other side.

Edge was a tall man: six feet three inches, and weighed a closely packed two hundred pounds. He was in his late thirties and the harsh experiences which had filled so many of these years could be seen in the deep lines that were carved across the skin of his face. It was a lean face and the skin was stretched taut between the high cheekbones and the firm jaw. He was colored dark brown by exposure to the elements—although his complexion had never been pale like that of his Scandinavian mother. For, like the jet black hair which he wore long enough to brush his shoulders and conceal the nape of his neck, it was drawn from the bloodline of his Mexican father. Set into the brown face were eyes of a light and icy blue between permanently narrowed lids. The nose was hawk-like and there was an unsubtle clue to the latent brutality of Edge in the thin-lipped mouthline. Several hours growth of bristles sprouted on his lower face, slightly longer and thicker above and to either side of his mouth to merely hint at a Mexican-style moustache.

Women other than Crystal Dickens had found the face of the man attractive. Many more had regarded it as ugly.

After perhaps a full five minutes of riding northwest from the San Juan River, he heard the clop of hooves behind him. The following horse was moving faster than his own, but then it was reined down and the paces were matched to maintain a gap of about a hundred yards. He did not turn and neither did he show any flicker of expression to reveal what he felt about the woman's decision to trail him.

Crystal Dickens was a brown-eyed, dark blonde woman of about thirty with a heart shaped face that was interestingly attractive rather than beautiful or even pretty. Her lips were full, the nose pert and the cheeks dimpled. Her complexion was unblemished and its color had shaded from pale to a pleasant tan in the time Edge had known her. Her build was slender but there were tell-tale signs that it would quickly thicken if she did not guard against putting on weight.

She was attired in much the same style of garb as Edge. Blue denim pants and check cotton shirt. Black riding boots, spurless, and grey Stetson. Her kerchief was red with white spots while his was plain grey. She carried no weapons. He had a Frontier Colt in a holster hung low from the right side of his gunbelt and tied to his thigh. And there was a straight razor in a sheath held to the nape of his neck by a beaded thong that was just visible above the kerchief. The stock of a Winchester jutted from a boot slung from the front right of his Western-style saddle. Both horses had bedrolls

4

lashed on to their backs behind the saddles. Top-coats and cooking and eating utensils were stowed in each roll.

They had made regular use of the bedrolls and their contents since riding out of the west Texas town of Irving many days ago, but Edge had drawn the revolver and rifle only to clean the guns. And he had taken out the razor merely to shave each morning.

It was mid-afternoon when they allowed their mounts to drink from the river reduced to a stream. And evening was hovering in the east, waiting to sweep across the desolate Colorado Plateau country in the wake of the set sun, when Edge brought his gelding to a halt on the crest of a rise. His hand moved to within three inches of where the frame of the Winchester showed at the mouth of the boot.

"What is it?" Crystal called, a quiver of fear in her voice.

From almost the first moment of their meeting, she had had reason to know that this man called Edge was never at ease—awake, and she was convinced, also when he was asleep. For most of the time, to the casual observer, he appeared almost lazily relaxed while he surveyed his surroundings with apparent bored indifference. But those slit-ted blue eyes of his missed nothing. And if they focused upon anything which might signal danger, he was instantly prepared to meet the threat. Just as now, on the top of the slope, he sat rigidly in the saddle. Peering ahead, his eyes were glinting in the failing light of the sun. Every muscle in his lean body poised to power him into whatever action was required if the threat became a reality.

The woman demanded a canter from her horse,

then slowed him down to a walk again as she closed with the man at the top of the slope.

"I asked what is it?" she said.

"A boat," he answered absently.

"A what?" She reined the stallion to a halt alongside the half breed and vented a gasp of surprise as she stared in the same direction as he. "Well, I'll be. . . . you're right."

"It's what I always try to be, lady," he growled. "This time it wasn't so hard."

From the point where the two sat their horses, the terrain stretched away northward as flat tableland for perhaps five miles before the horizon was delineated by a line of jagged ridges. The boat they peered at was the best part of a mile to the northwest, and the shack it dwarfed was clear to see in the soft, pinkish light of the setting sun.

It was a clinker built craft, maybe fifty feet long and twenty feet from keel to deck. The superstructure was only partially completed but there seemed to be sufficient lumber stacked on the aft deck to see the job done. The whole construction was held upright by an extensive arrangement of supporting beams.

The fact that the craft had been a long time in the making could be seen from the various degrees of weathering—the planking close to the keel looking like it was exposed to the elements for as long as the frame build shack close to the stern. The shack was single story and not large enough to have more than two rooms. There was a flatbed wagon parked beside it and two horses in a fenced corral out back. While Edge and Crystal Dickens watched, grey smoke began to curl up from the chimney.

"A boat in the middle of a desert?" the woman

muttered. "Whoever is building it must be out of his mind."

"And rich," Edge answered, heeling his horse forward with just one hand on the reins, the other staying close to the booted Winchester.

"Uh? Oh, yes. All that timber must have cost a fortune."

"And hauling it in, another fortune."

For a minute they rode side by side in silence. Then, her interest in the strange craft abated, Crystal cleared her throat.

"I was stupid. What I said back there. About being through with you. God knows how many miles from civilization. I promise to watch my language in future—if that's all right with you?"

He glanced at her and found she was eyeing him contritely and a little nervously. If the blow had marked her flesh, there had been time for the redness to fade.

"I never was going anywhere special, lady," he told her. "Figured you knew that."

"You never said."

"I never heard you ask."

He was concentrating his attention on the boat now, but heard the sharp intake of breath that revealed she was swallowing her anger. And then there was a new silence between them, and all around them save for the clop of slow moving hooves. Then the shack door creaked open and a man yelled:

"Hey there, you folks! Welcome to you! Glad to see you by here! Coffee's abubblin' and I'll be real pleased to throw some more eats in the cookin' pot!"

He was outside the shack by then, head craned forward and eyes squinting to see the newcomers

7

more clearly across the two hundred yard gap that separated them from him. He was an elderly man with grey hair and a bushy grey beard, short of stature and scrawny of frame. Hatless and bare footed, with a pair of ragged once-white pants flapping around his legs, he wore a torn and heavily soiled sleeveless undershirt fitting where it touched his torso. From the sound of his reedy voice and the slow way he moved, he seemed to be very old. When Edge and the woman had ridden close enough to see his lined and saggy flesh, weak and watery eyes and toothless gums, they placed him over seventy.

"Name's Attinger, folks," he greeted in the same gleeful tones. "Aristotle Attinger. Like it says up there. Mostly I'm called Telly for short. And I like that."

By *up there* he meant the board beamed stern of the boat where, to either side of the stout rudder shaft, was the crudely lettered: ARISTOTLE'S ARK.

The woman seemed on the point of losing control of a grin that would have expanded into a gust of laughter, until her eyes met Edge's for part of a second, and then the half-breed said to Attinger:

"Coffee sounds good, feller. I'm Edge. The lady is Miss Crystal Dickens."

The old-timer nodded vigorously after peering hard at both visitors and obviously approving of what he saw. "Food, too? It's just a mess of beans I'm havin' for supper tonight. You're welcome to put your animals in the corral out back. Some hay out there. And water in the trough."

"Obliged," Edge said as he slid from the saddle

and Attinger swung around and limped back into the shack.

Remembering the ice-cold look in the half-breed's eyes, the woman had no difficulty in curbing her instinct to laugh at the crazy old-timer and his grandiosely-named landlocked boat. And said nothing until they had led their horses to the rear of the shack and were in the corral, unfastening the cinches.

"You don't find this whole thing ridiculous, Edge?" she asked coldly.

"Maybe a little more so than what you did, lady," the half-breed answered. "Did I laugh at you before accepting your hospitality?"

She scowled. "By that, I suppose you mean before I gave you ten thousand dollars and myself? No, you didn't laugh. You slapped me around." She tentatively touched the place on her face where the most recent blow had landed. "And I'll tell you something for nothing, Edge. For choice, I'd rather be laughed at."

"You had the choice, lady," he told her as they carried their gear out of the corral and replaced the bar across the opening in the fence. "Stay in or pull out. And you knew the rules from the start. If you stayed, you ran the risk of getting beat."

She pouted and snapped, "It was never just like a game to me."

Edge grinned at the woman. "Way I recall it, the first time we laid eyes on each other it turned out to be a matter of stud poke her."

"You arrogant pig!" she snarled, and moved ahead of him to go into the shack.

Crystal Dickens had run a lot of risks to find the man called Edge—leaving New York City and carrying ten thousand dollars cash which she had reason to believe belonged to him. She got lucky and the two came together in the saloon of the small Texas town of Irving, where violence erupted. Men died, and without wanting it, Edge found himself the owner of the saloon with the woman his partner. The violence of that first night spilled over into the following days and because of the bitter experiences of the long past, the half-breed stoically accepted the inevitable outcome of trouble that was not of his making. And rode out of Irving to pick up again his life as a drifter—without a penny of the ten thousand dollars which had never really been his. But, by her own choice, he left with the woman who had taken so many risks to bring it to him.

"Guess you folks think I'm crazy as a loon? Like everyone else around here?"

There was just one room in the twenty by twenty shack—a combination living room, bedroom and kitchen, furnished with just the bare essentials of daily life.

Attinger was at a stove in a corner, stirring a pot from which arose the appetizing aroma of cooked beans. The woman had dragged the small table over alongside the narrow bed and was in process of pouring coffee into two tin mugs. Then she sat down on the bed and scalded her tongue when she tried to drink her coffee. Pointedly ignoring the half-breed as he set his gear down on the floor beside hers, she asked:

"Are you a Mormon, Mr. Attinger?"

"A what, young lady?"

"A Mormon. Religious people who had to leave the east and settle here in Utah."

"No, no I ain't," the old man answered. "I ain't

got no religious label. Just a belief in the Virgin Mary, Jesus Christ and the Lord God Almighty."

Edge had taken his eating and drinking utensils from his bedroll and now carried them to the table, gripping the back of the shack's single chair and dragging it behind him on the way. He poured coffee into his mug.

"Awhile back, up in Wyoming, I met with some people who figured it was time for the Second Coming, feller," he said.

Attinger turned to look hard at the half-breed, obviously ready to get angry if he suspected he was the butt of ridicule. But Edge was impassive as he sipped at the hot, strong coffee.

"Lots of folks get visions, young man. And I ain't sayin' there ain't many that ain't crazy. Or just says things out of spite or trickery or some such. But I ain't got no kinda axe to grind. And I don't stand to make no money outta what I'm doin'. That coffee all right?"

"It's fine, Mr. Attinger," the woman assured.

"Just the opposite, feller," Edge said.

"What?"

"It's costing you a bundle to build that boat outside."

"Sure enough is, young man. But it don't matter. Because I can afford it. And even if I couldn't, I'd have gotten the money somehow. When the call comes from where mine did, a man just has to answer it. Pass your plates, folks. Grub's ready."

Edge remained seated and the woman grudgingly took both tin plates across to the stove, where Attinger ladled a heap of beans on to each of them. Then, as she delivered them to the table, the old man struck a match and lit a kerosene

11

lamp hanging from the center of the ceiling. The darkness of night retreated beyond the walls of the shack. A wind began to whine softly through the supporting timbers holding the ark upright. And dust was blown in through the doorway of the shack. The old-timer crossed to creak the door closed, leaned against it, folded his arms and grinned through his beard—looking like a man who had achieved something much prized.

"Aren't you going to eat, Mr. Attinger?" the woman asked.

He shook his head. "Suddenly I ain't hungry, young lady. But you two folks, you eat hearty. Hear that wind? Buildin' up, seems to me. This could be it."

"Be what?" Crystal posed, and wrinkled her nose.

"The new flood," Edge put in and was aware of the apprehension which had gripped the woman seated opposite him.

With the door of the windowless shack closed, the place smelled bad. The stench of the building's neglected and decaying fabric and of the old man's foul breath and unwashed flesh had permeated through the atmosphere all the time, of course. But the cooling fresh air of evening and the aromas of brewing coffee and cooked beans had masked the stink until now. When the increasingly forceful north wind was barred access, the coffee had ceased to steam and the pot of beans was off the stove.

"That's right, that's right," Attinger said in high excitement. "And I got a proposition for you folks. That'll make you the luckiest young couple in this entire bad, bad world. She ain't properly finished

12

yet. Ain't fitted out like they say. But she'll float, you can take old Telly's word on that. She'll float and she'll be stable in any kind of storm. And when the waters go down she'll land us safely wherever it pleases the good Lord to have us."

Crystal had raised a spoonful of beans to her lips. And now she wrinkled her nose again and held the attitude for a stretched second while her eyes expressed a tacit query to Edge.

The half-breed bent his head low, to bring his face within an inch or so of the heap of beans on his plate.

"When the rains start, folks will come down here from Ventura," Aristotle Attinger went on in the same mood of triumph. "All them folks that had me marked as a crazy man for doin' what the good Lord told me to. And if any of them make it before they're engulfed by the flood, they won't have to beg to let me have them come aboard. I told them that. If they make it, it'll be a sign from the good Lord that they are the chosen ones. Just like you young people showin' up here is a sign. Listen. Listen to that wind. You hear any rain yet?"

The old man's eyes had been squeezed tightly closed while he delivered the monologue. Now he snapped them open and his mood suffered an abrupt change: to fear. Not of the man and the woman who were peering at him from either side of the table. Rather he was gripped by terror of having certain victory snatched away and replaced by irrevocable defeat.

"I hear you talking up a storm is all, feller," Edge said evenly. "And I smell something bad. Before anyone's eaten any beans."

13

"You think he tried to poison us, Edge?" the woman asked tensely. And squeezed a hand to her throat.

The half-breed rose slowly to his feet.

"No!" the old-timer blurted and unfolded his arms, to stretch out his hands in a gesture of innocence. "No, it's not poison! Just a potion to make people sleep. A medicine I bought from an old Paiute squaw! It wouldn't harm you none! I'm a true believer in the good Lord and I live by the Commandments he gave to Moses! I wouldn't knowingly harm any livin' creature! Thou shalt not kill! I just wanted to . . ."

Edge took a step toward the blabbering old man and spoke in the silence that followed the curtailment of his explanation. "Some rules are made to be broken, feller." He gripped the fingers of his right hand with those of his left and jerked. The knuckles cracked louder than the howling wind in the night outside. "Easy as an old-timer's bones."

"Edge!" Crystal called shrilly, as Attinger groaned in dismay, whirled awkwardly, freed the catch, flung open the door and lunged outside. Dust billowed across the threshold as the half-breed stepped into the doorway and halted.

There was no rain and the light of the half moon was bright from a sky ragged with thin white clouds scudding fast in the grip of the norther that gusted across the Colorado Plateau.

For long moments, while Attinger wailed in competition with the sound of the wind through the framework of timber, swirling dust drew a veil across the scene out front of the shack.

Then there was a lull in the storm. And Edge saw the old man come to a staggering halt and drop hard to his knees, in front of two long coated horsemen.

Both riders were leveling cocked revolvers at the towering form of the half-breed starkly silhouetted against the lamplit doorway.

Attinger vented another shrill wail of despairing, demented terror.

And the mounted man on the right drawled, "What's the idea, mister? Scarin' my Pa this way!"

Edge was poised to draw his Colt and blast at the men as he threw himself back into the shack. If it proved necessary. But his voice revealed no hint of tension when he replied: "On account of the beans, feller."

"Beans?" the younger rider on the left growled, and the gun in his hand exploded.

The bullet sprayed wood splinters from the inside of the open door.

"Vince, you fool!" the older man yelled. Then: "Mister, we—"

Edge crouched, drew the Frontier Colt, cocked the hammer and squeezed the trigger.

The younger rider shrieked: "Pa, I never—"

And both men hurled themselves out of their saddles as the bullet from the half-breed's gun cracked between them and imbedded itself in the stern of the boat.

Edge was inside the shack by then, his back pressed against the cover of the wall.

"My God, not again!" Crystal Dickens moaned.

"Get over here!" Edge snarled at her, and swung his revolver to aim at the kerosene lamp.

The woman ignored his order, and threw herself full length along the bed which reeked of the old-timer's neglected body.

"No shootin', Augie!" Telly Attinger shouted

15

desperately and Edge stayed his finger on the trigger—and inched his head to the side to risk a glance outside. "Put that gun away, Vince! No other folks must die on account of what I been told to do by the good Lord!"

The old man was still on his knees and he swung his head between the two men crouched to either side of him. Then he directed a pleading gaze over his shoulder toward the lamplit doorway. Next, he sank his rump on to his heels, clasped his hands together and threw back his head to tilt his face to the cloud streaked sky. The wind howled to mask the mumbled words of his prayer, and eddies of dust blurred the scene between the shack and the stern of the boat.

"I didn't mean it, Pa!" Vince wailed. "My finger slipped and she just went off!"

Augie yelled, "You hear that, mister? The shot was an accident! Me and my boy don't want no trouble with you!"

Edge tried to penetrate the stinging dust with one slitted, glinting eye around the doorpost. He glimpsed the two men with their revolvers still drawn, but no longer held in a threatening attitude. He rasped, "Holster those guns and never draw them against me again. Won't need to trouble you then."

The father and son looked anxiously at each other, then complied with the half-breed's demand.

Edge holstered his own Colt and swung on to the threshold of the shack again.

Crystal Dickens remained face down on the bed, silent and unmoving.

The old-timer continued to pray.

"Yeah, beans," the half-breed said in a level

tone, as if the exchange of gunshots had never happened. "The old man didn't eat any, but they're the reason he got the wind up."

"What the frig you talkin' about?" Augie Attinger snarled.

The man's short-tempered response nudged Edge close to the stage where he was likely to draw the Colt again. But the two men staring at him were unaware of this, failing to notice that after he had shrugged his shoulders, his right hand was just a fraction of an inch away from the butt of the holstered revolver.

"Because of the draught he put in them."

Chapter Two

"WHAT'S he sayin', Pa?" Vince growled. "I thought it was just gramps was supposed to be off his rocker!"

The bed creaked and the woman's footfalls sounded on the hard-packed dirt floor of the shack. And Telly Attinger's son and grandson looked at her in surprise when her silhouetted form appeared beside Edge in the lighted doorway.

"Who's she?" Vince asked huskily.

"Far as you're concerned, kid, just hips that pass in the night," the half-breed drawled.

"The old man tried to poison us," Crystal said dully.

"He did what?" Augie countered, shocked. Then hugged his open coat around his body. "Look, can we all come inside and talk about this? It ain't exactly comfortable out here."

"Be his guest," Edge answered, pointing to the praying man. "But don't eat any of his food."

He withdrew into the shack, picked up the pot of cooled coffee and placed it on the stove. Crystal returned to sit on the side of the bed, pale beneath her recent tan. She stared down at the congealing beans on the two plates.

Outside, Augie Attinger instructed: "Take care of the horses, son. Cut out that prayin' crap and do some explainin', Pa!"

There were muttered responses from his father and son, then he entered the shack with the dejected old-timer immediately behind him.

Augie was close to fifty and perhaps because of the old man's beard and crinkled skin, it was difficult to see any family resemblance between the two. He was a head taller with a strong looking build. He had short clipped black hair with some grey in the long sideburns and blue eyes set too close together. He had the lined and stained skin of a man who worked in the outdoors and the gnarled hands of one whose work was hard. Beneath the white duster, which he took off after closing the door on the storm, he was dressed Western style in faded blue denim. There was maybe a two day growth of bristles on his jaw and throat, and his skin and eyes looked ravaged by long and uncomfortable travel.

But he was able to generate sour hardness into the gaze he shared between Edge and the woman as he opened:

"Tell you my side first. That's my son outside and this here is my Pa. Year ago he sold the family business in Omaha. River freight business. Seventeen steamboats operatin' out of Omaha, Kansas City, Saint Louis and Memphis. Coverin' every stretch of the Mississippi and Missouri which can take a sternwheeler. Got twenty-five thousand dollars for the whole kit and caboodle and took off for parts unknown. While me and my boy were down in New Orleans fixin' to open up there. Took Vince and me the whole year to track him down."

Augie paused as the door was opened to admit his son and the louder sounds of the storm. Then he continued:

"Ain't none of that any of your business. Mister. Ma'am. But I told you so you'll know we ain't here to do nothin' that'll cause you trouble. And, I guess, in hopes that you'll return the favor and level with me."

"What's it all about, Pa?" Vince asked, after shedding his dust scattering hat and coat, all the while casting surreptitious glances at the still shaken Crystal Dickens.

He was in his early twenties and his features were an immature version of those of the man who fathered him. Youth had allowed him to stand up better to the rigors of the long trail and what signs of weariness did show failed to detract from his good looks.

"If you hush up, boy, maybe we'll find out," Augie told him.

Edge poured himself a coffee and said, "You'll need to bring in your own stuff if you're counting on staying."

"We'll do without for now," Augie said.

Edge nodded and held out the coffee pot toward the woman, who shook her head and explained, "This gentleman and I are just passing through, Mr. Attinger. Your father invited us inside and offered us food." She grimaced and pushed her plate of cold beans away from in front of her. "We were just about to eat it when we noticed it smelled bad. Then he started to rant about having a vision and said he'd put some Indian potion in the food to make us sleep. Mr. Edge here

20

didn't take kindly to hearing that. Then your father ran outside. Which was when you arrived."

Edge sipped his coffee.

Augie and Vince Attinger stood with their backs to the door, holding their hats and coats. Augie nodded several times while the woman was speaking. And Vince stared incredulously at his grandfather who had retreated to a corner of the shack and was pressing himself into the angle of the walls. He looked like a frightened child expecting imminent punishment.

"It's true," the old-timer whined. "To put them to sleep is what I—"

"Hush up, you old fool," Augie said, softly but with authority. He sighed, looking suddenly more weary as he shared a gaze between the woman and the half-breed. "We heard up in Ventura how he was spendin' the money. Wastin' it on this crazy scheme to build a boat in the middle of the desert. Like Noah and his ark. But how he—" Augie glared at the cowering old-timer now. "—figured to load it with people instead of animals. Young people who'd be able to breed a new generation after the flood drowned everyone else in the world. My God, what a—"

"Yes, boy!" the old man in the corner exclaimed, and came erect. "Your God and my God and everyone's God! It was He who told me what to do! He who told me to come to this place to build the ark! Here in the pure country, away from the corrupt masses! I was told that the chosen would come to me! But they're late! The time is ever drawin' near! My work is almost complete! I went lookin'! In Ventura! But the people there only laughed, the fools! So I have abandoned them to their fate! And the good Lord has begun to direct the true chosen to me! Listen! Listen to the start of the storm that will destroy the corrupt world! And praise Him who has led you here! You will be saved! Saved to breed a new, better race of human beings!"

While the old-timer shrieked the fanatical words at them, his audience remained silent. Vince appeared uncomprehending. Augie expressed disgust. Crystal showed something close to pity. Edge was impassive as he rolled and lit a thin cigarette.

Then Augie swung around and took a long, menacing stride toward his father, which was enough to drive the old-timer back into fearful silence. And Augie sighed with exhausted relief.

"All right, Pa," he said softly. "I guess we all know as much as we need to know now."

"Except for one thing," the youngest Attinger put in sourly.

"What's that, boy?" his father asked.

Vince stared hard at the now subdued old-timer as he answered, "How much money has he got left? And where is it?"

Augie got angry again, and this time directed it at his son. "I said all we need to know *for now*, boy!" he snarled. "That's family business and there's no call to talk that in front of strangers!"

He snatched a glance at Edge and Crystal, seeing indifference on the lean features of the half-breed, but glimpsing a flicker of interest on the face of the woman before she averted her eyes.

"I ain't gonna tell you!" the old-timer challenged. "I sold what was mine and I'm entitled to the money I got for it."

"Pa?" Vince rasped.

"Hush up, boy," Augie snapped as he shared a glower between his father and his son. Then he instructed, "Go bring in our stuff from where you left it, Vincent."

The youngest Attinger went grudgingly out into the night through which the wind was blowing as strongly as ever. The moon was still bright above the swirling dust and there was no smell of dampness in the air.

"Like to know something, feller?" Edge asked after the door had banged closed behind Vince.

"Long as it don't amount to pokin' your nose in Attinger business, mister," Augie allowed, and crossed the room to take the old-timer's mug down from a shelf above the stove. "All right to drink from this?"

Edge nodded. "Where's Ventura and what's there?"

Augie poured himself a coffee and sipped it while he answered. "Well, I'd say it's about five miles north of here, Mr. . . ?"

"He's called Edge," the woman supplied. "I'm Crystal Dickens. And you have no need to worry about us having designs on whatever money your father has left."

Augie was intrigued by the bitterness of the woman's tone. But then he shook his head and went on to Edge, "Guess it could be called a town. Mostly tents on silver claims. And a lot of claims that are abandoned. Only frame buildings are a store and saloon and a railroad depot."

"Railroad depot?" Crystal asked eagerly.

Augie shrugged and nodded. "That's right, ma'am. At the end of a spur off the Denver and Rio Grande track. Just the one train goes back and forth haulin' the ore. But they carry passengers in

23

the caboose. Vince and me rode down from Colorado Junction aboard the train."

His son came in through the dust-filled doorway, heavily laden with two saddles and bedrolls.

The old-timer pleaded, "You folks don't want to leave for Ventura tonight. What with the storm and all. Even if the rain don't come, it won't be no picnic ridin' into the teeth of a norther."

"This place ain't exactly well equipped to handle this many house guests, old man," Augie growled.

"But there's plenty of room aboard the ark," Telly Attinger countered triumphantly. "I got berths for better than forty people. You and me and the boy can go aboard and these folks can bed down here in the shack." There was a desperate plea in his weak and watery eyes as he looked from the woman to Edge and back again. "And if the storm blows out and the rains don't come, you can head for Ventura in the mornin'."

"That sounds like a good plan, Mister Attinger," Crystal allowed. "And I'd certainly like to accept your invitation. Edge is free to do as he pleases."

The half-breed dropped the butt of his cigarette in the pot of cold and congealed beans. And he said sardonically, "Never accept a favor without returning it, feller. I'll bed down under your roof. In exchange, I'll cook breakfast."

The unsubtle reference to the attempted poisoning was lost on the old-timer, whose happy relief sounded in a child-like giggle—which was in contrast to the disgruntled snort vented by his son as he picked up his own saddle and bedroll from where Vince had dumped them on the floor. Then, with a kind of grudging attempt to be civil, he said, "All right, Mister Edge, ma'am. This is my

24

father's place and he's entitled to have you stay if you want. And hearin' that weather out there, I reckon I wouldn't have you ride through it if it was up to me. Come on, Pa. Vince. Let's go take a look aboard that crazy contraption outside."

Without waiting for responses, he pushed open the door and stepped across the threshold. His son glanced at Crystal and received a coy smile in return before he followed. Telly Attinger held back a few moments to say:

"I ain't thinkin' you folks would, but if anyone had a mind to look for cash in the house, they wouldn't find it."

Then he went out and the door closed behind him.

Edge grinned coldly at the woman. "Figure you're thinking you've already found what you're looking for, lady?"

She rose from the bed and went to get her bed-roll. "Except for that crack about hips passing in the night, it's been a long time since you showed you wanted me," she answered in a tone as icy as his expression. She unfurled the roll. "I'm sleeping on the floor here. The bed stinks."

She took off just her boots and kerchief before getting under the blanket. Edge put some cord-wood into the stove, then turned down the lamp wick, dragged his gear across the floor, pushed the table away and stretched out on his back on the bed. He kept his boots on and tipped his hat forward over his face. His right hand rested only inches away from where the Winchester jutted from the boot on the saddle.

The stale smell of the bedding was as bad as the woman had implied but the half-breed was able to endure it with indifference—as he had learned to endure so much that other "normal" people regarded as insufferably repugnant.

Death and destruction. Squalor and loneliness. Deprivation and hatred. Agony and anguish.

During the early years, when he had been Josiah C. Hedges, he experienced perhaps less than his fair share of the cruelties of life. In the days of his youth and young adulthood on the small farm in Iowa, he lived with his happily married parents and his kid brother Jamie.

Just one memory of those far off times could today, if he allowed it, swamp his mind with bitter thoughts. While playing with a gun which should not have been loaded, he fired a shot that made Jamie a cripple. But he chose never to voluntarily recall that summer afternoon in the yard of the farm on the prairie. And it came vividly and unbidden to mind only on those occasions when anyone leveled a gun at him.

By the time the War between the States came, the brothers' Mexican father and Scandinavian mother were peacefully dead and perhaps Josiah should not have left the farm to become a lieutenant and then a captain in the Union cavalry. But he felt compelled to answer President Lincoln's call for volunteers and in the long years of fighting the Confederacy he experienced the very darkest side of life—the depths of inhumanity to which men could plunge in the treatment of their fellows. He experienced and learned the lessons of survival in such situations, and then was ready and anxious to forget what he had been taught in this hard school when the war was finally over.

But this was not to be. For when he returned to Iowa it was to discover Jamie brutally murdered and the farmstead a burnt-out ruin. And it was during his search for those responsible that he became Edge. He took a new name for the different kind of man he was. Different, because in tracking down and killing Jamie's murderers and in the grueling years that were to ensue, he was what he had been in the war—but without a uniform and a cause to place his actions and reactions within the law.

It was the killing of a man not involved in the carnage on the Iowa farm which placed him on the wanted list in Kansas. And a cruel fate which set him on an endless trail with death, his invisible companion and violence threatening to explode at every stopping place.

Over the years of riding the trail that crisscrossed the states and territories of his native country and sometimes took him south into Mexico, he had attempted from time to time to set down new roots and to cement relationships with others. But always he had failed—forced to admit defeat to the ruling fate which demanded he not be like other men.

From out of the violent years, two memories could be recalled as vividly as finding the buzzard ravaged corpse of Jamie: The manner in which Beth, his wife, had died on another farmstead—this one up in the Dakotas; and, more recently, the granting by a government man in New York City, of an amnesty on the old killing in Kansas so long ago.

The death of his wife had affected him deeply—forced him finally to realize that he was doomed to a life of a loner and a loser.

The pardon on the murder charge . . . ? A temptation he willed himself to ignore.

"If you really want me, I'll stay with you,

27

Edge," Crystal Dickens said softly in the wake of the storm blowing itself into extinction.

"I don't want anything, lady," he said into the darkness of the crown of his hat. "Sometimes need things is all."

"And when you're through needing it, it's nothing but a burden to you!" she answered bitterly.

"Not food or drink or clothes or a horse or a bedroll or a gun, lady."

"But people are!"

"No, lady. People don't bother me unless they're in the way of something I need. But if they stay around me, they have to be responsible for what happens to them."

She was as silent as the now still night for long moments. Then she said flatly, "You know what you are, Edge?"

"Yeah, I know what I am."

"You only think you do. What you really are is two hundred odd pounds of self pity stacked higher than six feet."

He grimaced into the underside of his hat. "You're wrong, lady. That's what I used to be. Before I ran out of pity for other people. Now I'm just somebody trying to stay alive and not get hurt in the process."

"Staying alive for what?" she challenged.

The secret grimace changed to an unseen grin. "Who the hell knows, lady? Maybe if the old-timer's flood had come tonight, we would all have known that answer."

There was another stretched second of silence. Then the beat of galloping hooves receding from the rear of the shack. A revolver shot cracked out front and above roof level from the deck of the ark.

"You bastard, you killed Pa!" Vince Attinger shrieked in an hysterical tone.

Another shot exploded while Edge and the woman were ripping off their blankets and rising.

The hoofbeats continued to recede without any break in the regular galloping cadence.

Crystal reached the door first and threw it open. She came to a halt as a third gunshot sounded, then grunted in pain as Edge shouldered her out of the way and crossed the threshold, working the lever action of the Winchester.

The youngest Attinger was skylined on the transom of the ark: Squatting on his haunches and holding the revolver in both hands, forearms resting on the big tiller to take useless aim at the distant rider.

He fired a third shot.

Edge yelled: "He's out of range, kid!"

The series of clicks as the revolver hammer was thumbed back could be heard. The galloping hooves had faded from earshot. Vince Attinger looked as if he was about to send a fourth bullet cracking uselessly out into the night. But then he sobbed and his forehead fell forward to rest on his wrists. A moment later he jerked upright and stared down at the half-breed.

"We gotta get after him, mister!" he cried. "He knifed his own son in the back, the rotten bastard!"

Edge ignored the young Attinger and went around to the rear of the shack. As he checked on the horses in the corral, he heard Crystal Dickens ask if Vince was sure his father was dead. When he returned to the front of the building, the woman paused halfway up the ladder to look back and down at him.

"Well, aren't you going after him?" she demanded.

Edge eased the hammer gently forward and canted the rifle to his shoulder as he replied, "He stole my horse."

From below decks in the ark, Vince yelled, "He's still alive! Pa's still breathin'!"

The woman said, "Perhaps it's best we see what we can do to help here." And she clambered up the remaining rungs of the ladder.

Edge rasped through clenched teeth as he followed her. "No sweat, lady. I've seen him and I've laid in his bed. And ain't no way that old sonofabitch is going to get clean away."

Chapter Three

AUGIE Attinger had located what was left of the money his father got for the family business. It had been hidden in a compartment beneath a section of decking in the galley of the ark.

But his father had found him only moments after the secret cache came to light. And now Augie lay face down across the deckboards he had removed, one hand hanging limply into the empty compartment, with a carving knife buried almost to the hilt in his back—low down and left of the spine, in the region of his kidneys.

A kerosene lamp was lit and Vince Attinger and Crystal Dickens were down on their hands and knees to either side of the knifed man: he was peering anxiously into the bristled face, and she was exploring with fingertips for a pulse in his neck.

"He's barely alive, Edge," she reported.

"What we gonna do?" Vince asked helplessly.

Edge placed his Winchester on a table, stooped down, rested one hand in the small of Augie's back and with the other drew the knife from the flesh. Blood spurted, and the woman swung away, venting a sound of nausea but keeping the vomit trapped in her throat.

"Easier for him now than if he comes out of it," the half-breed murmured, and abruptly was gentle in the way he eased the shirt and undershirt out from under the belt and top of the pants. Blood continued to flow, but had become an ooze rather than a surge, from the inch long wound in the smooth white flesh.

"Check if the old-timer thought to have any medical supplies aboard," Edge instructed as he rose. "If he did, clean the wound and cover it. If he didn't, do the best you can with what's available."

"Where you goin,' mister?" Vince asked. "Hitch the team to the wagon, feller."

"Moving him could kill him," Crystal warned, her features still contorted by the taste of bile in her mouth.

"Figure with a wound that deep he'll die where he is if we don't move him. Chance that if he lives as far as Ventura and there's a doctor there, he could make it. He's your father, kid. What do you want to do?"

Vince, his eyes filled with desperation, switched his gaze several times between the impassive face of Edge and the unmoving features of his father. Then he rose to his feet and nodded.

"I think we should try to get him to Ventura, mister. That's gotta be better than just sittin' around here watchin' him die."

The half-breed gave no acknowledgment. He simply retrieved his rifle and went out of the galley, up a stairway and through a hatch on to the deck of the ark, then down the ladder and out to the corral at the rear of the shack.

He worked with methodical, practiced ease to put the team in the traces of the flatbed wagon, and then he drove it around to the foot of the ladder. Before going aboard the ark again, he carried the bed mattress and his own and the woman's bedrolls out of the shack and arranged them crossways behind the wagon seat.

When he returned to the galley, Augie Attinger's wound had been bound with lengths of clean rag which already showed an ugly crimson stain of seeping blood. Then, after Edge had slumped the wounded man carefully over his shoulder and carried him gently out on to deck and down the ladder to the wagon, the white dressing across Augie's back was completely soaked—even dripping.

"He's bleeding like a stuck pig, Edge!" Crystal said, and looked again as if she were about to throw up.

"If he stops bleeding it'll maybe mean he's dead," the half-breed growled and signaled for the mournful-faced Vince to help him load the comatose Augie aboard the wagon. "Like for one of you to ride in the rear with him. Keep him from jolting around too much."

"I'll do it," Vince volunteered.

"And I'll stay here," the woman added as Edge dropped from the tailgate to the ground. When the cold eyes of the half-breed glanced at her she augmented quickly, "Maybe he'll come back. Sure to if it starts to rain."

"Suit yourself, lady."

He went into the shack again, came out with his saddle and tossed it up into the rear of the wagon.

"You, too?" Crystal asked when he had climbed on to the seat and taken up the reins.

"What?"

"You'll come back?"

He glanced pointedly at the totally cloudless sky. "It ain't going to rain, lady. And all I need is to get my horse."

He took off the brake, growled a command to the team and jerked on the reins to turn the horses and wagon. Not looking over his shoulder, he headed his charges on to the clearly defined trail which had been made by many two-way trips between the shack and Ventura to bring the lumber out here.

After a few minutes, when Vince had rearranged the bedding to make his father as comfortable as possible, the youngest Attinger said, "How is it a man can stick a knife in his own father, mister?"

The team knew the way and Edge asked for no more than a gentle walk to keep the wounded Augie from jolting around too much. He had rolled a cigarette and struck a match on the seat to light it as Vince's questions interrupted a line of thought concerned with Crystal Dickens.

"Pointed end first, feller," he answered flatly.

Vince vented a choked, angry sound. Then groaned, "I ain't in no mood to listen to smart talk!"

"Nor me to answer dumb questions," Edge countered with no tone of rancor. "Way it looked, your Pa was fixing to rob your Grandpa who ain't exactly right in the head. He should have figured the risk and taken more care to cover his back."

"You don't know anythin' about it!" Vince snarled.

"So tell me, kid."

"Why the hell should I?"

Edge shrugged. "We have a five mile ride ahead of us. You were the one who started to talk. I'll be just as happy with my own thoughts."

Which was a lie, he acknowledged to himself as he spat over the side of the seat.

For awhile, Vincent Attinger stayed quiet. And the half-breed attempted to block from his mind any reflections about Crystal Dickens by paying more attention than usual to the brightly moonlit terrain spread out on all sides. He sensed that the distraught youngster in back of him was engaged in an anguished battle to bear the silence.

"Why you doin' this, mister?" came the words at length. "We're nothin' to you? Gramps stole your horse and has a pile of money. Why you takin' the time to help me and Pa?"

"My business."

For a longer period now, just the clop of hooves, roll of wheelrims and creak of timber broke the silence of the Utah night. Then Vince revealed he had spent the time in constructive thought.

"I reckon that means you're all right, mister."

"It does?" He arced the cigarette butt out to the side of the trail.

"You're in this for money. But honest money. A finder's fee. If you had wanted the whole lot, you'd—you and the lady—would have taken off after Gramps, soon as he made a run for it."

"Uh, uh," Edge muttered. "And how do I stand to make my trouble worthwhile, feller?"

"We can work out somethin', mister. And if Pa pulls through, he'll go along with it, you can be sure of that."

"Something else I have to be sure of first."

35

"What's that?"

"The money your grandfather has doesn't rightfully belong to him, kid."

"No it don't!" Vince snapped.

"I been to Omaha already. I don't want to go again."

"Damnit, it's the truth, mister!" He paused to control his thoughts and his tone. "Look, I'll tell you about it. Gramps started the steamboat business way back before the war. Him and Pa and Ma were headin' for Oregon on a wagon train but I was born in Saint Jo. And while Ma was gettin' over havin' me, Gramps figured out the family would have a better chance of makin' it big in the middle of the country instead of out west.

"And the way it turned out, we did. They worked real hard to get things started and when I was old enough, I did my fair share. We never got rich in money in the bank because whenever we made any, it went toward buyin' more boats or openin' up depots in other cities. But we all lived pretty good. And it was always took for granted that when Gramps retired or died, Pa and me would get the business for ourselves. Damnit it, mister, we done all the work after Gramps got bit by the religion bug. But we never took him serious, the way he sat around the house all day readin' the Bible. Pa figured it was just he was gettin' senile and ready to die. He never did even think about gettin' somethin' down on paper to prove him and me had legal right to a share in the business. Until he upped and sold the whole thing while we was away down river.

"Mister, what I'm tellin' you is the whole truth."

"Figure it has to be," Edge allowed.

"Uh?"

"You just told me your grandfather has legal right to every cent he was paid for the steamboat business."

"No!" Vince blurted. "Pa says no. He says there ain't a proper court of law in the country that wouldn't find we have a right to a share."

"He didn't get stabbed in the back in any courtroom, feller," the half-breed pointed out.

"Damnit, the crazy old bastard goaded Pa into searchin' for the money, mister!" Vince retorted. "Soon as we got aboard that lousy boat, Gramps started in to cause trouble. Said how there was better than half the cash still left. But that we'd never get a red cent of it. Because it was too well hid and soon as the flood came, he was gonna burn it—that when everyone else in the world was drowned, there wouldn't be any need of money."

He sighed and calmed down. "I ain't sure what happened then. I was beat and I bedded down. Heard Pa come in the cabin a little later. Then I woke up and saw he wasn't there. Went lookin' for him and found him like you saw. Then heard the horse. And went near as crazy as the old bastard is."

Edge said nothing and Vince allowed perhaps a full minute to pass before he asked, "Well, mister?"

"Well what, kid?"

"You agree me and Pa have a rightful claim to a share of the money?"

"It matter what I think?"

"Sure as hell does. Even if he lives, Pa ain't gonna be able to go lookin' for Gramps for a long time. And I'd like to stay with him until I know what's gonna happen, one way or the other. Like I

37

said more or less already, I trust you. But I won't have no money to pay you until Gramps is found."

"No sweat about me finding him, kid. He's stole my horse."

"And our money, damnit!" Vince blurted, sounding close to tears.

Edge nodded and clucked his tongue against the roof of his mouth. "Guess that puts us just where the old-timer wanted us, rain or not."

"What the hell are you talkin' about?"

The half-breed grinned wryly toward the distant lights of Ventura as he drawled, "All in the same boat."

Chapter Four

THE mining community of Ventura was sited in a hollow between two pieces of high ground. To the west was a sheer cliff rising to more than a hundred feet and to the east, the rock sloped upward in a much more gentle incline.

The route from the tableland to the south lay down the shallowest drop of all to end between the railroad depot and a two storey building with a painted sign proclaiming it as "Regan's Place." From this point, a trail and single track railroad ran north, arrow straight across level ground for at least a mile before both curved out of sight around a bluff to the east.

Scattered to either side of the railroad and the trail were close to fifty tents of many shapes, none of them large enough to hold more than three people with the minimum of their possessions.

There were holes in the ground all over the area, both within the confines of the tent town and beyond—those dug in the east slope and pocking the base of the cliff to the west, obviously having been exhausted of metal bearing rock.

All the tents were in darkness and there was just one lit lamp midway along the railroad depot building—illuminating a sign which read: "Ventura—Silver Capital of Utah."

Directly across the three spur lines and the broad street, light spilled dimly from over the batwing doors and the flanking windows of Regan's Place. But after Edge had drawn the wagon to a halt in front of the crumbling stoop of the combination store and saloon, there were no sounds from inside to back up the lamplight's indication that the place was open.

The half-breed, with Winchester held in the crook of an arm, rapped his booted feet on the stoop boarding and halted to look in over the batwings.

A girl greeted, "Howdy, mister."

A sleeping man started to snore, grunted and settled back into peaceful rest.

And another man growled, "I'm just about to close up, stranger."

Edge pushed through the doors and asked, "Looking for a doctor."

The girl laughed as if it took a lot of effort and answered, "You're the healthiest man I seen around here in a long time."

She was no older than twenty. Thin rather than slim, with small breasts and a waist that was hardly defined above her hips. The make-up on her pretty face had run and smudged, and her mouse-brown hair was tangled and looked greasy.

She stood with her back to the bar, a cup of cooled coffee in her right hand. Her stance was a match for the drunken tone of her voice, the set of her slack mouth, and the contents of the tilted cup dripping steadily to the floor.

The man who wanted to close the place was behind the bar to her right. He was fat and fifty and tired—not just from the work of a long day. He had a grey moustache and an arc of grey hair above each ear. His eyes were small and flesh crowded and there was a sullen pout to the set of his thick lips above a series of double chins. He was a head taller than the girl's five and a half feet.

In front of the barcounter, which ran along the side of the thirty by thirty saloon, were a dozen tables each ringed by four mismatched chairs. In one darkened corner of the room, on the fringe of the light from two ceiling-hung lamps, the sleeping man was sprawled across a table, his right hand fisted around an empty glass and his left clutching an almost empty whiskey bottle. His face was turned away from the entrance and a derby hat was balanced on his head. All that Edge could make out about him was that he was tall and thin.

"Comes from clean living," Edge answered gazing directly at the bartender. "Does this town have one or not, feller?"

The man stabbed a stubby finger at the sleeping drunk. "That's Gerry McArthur, stranger. He pulls bad teeth, lances boils and cleans up cuts. Personally I wouldn't let him jerk a wood splinter outta my little finger."

"How far to a doctor that can be trusted, feller?"

"Colorado Junction up where this line joins with the D. and R.G. track. Two days fast horse ridin'. Few hours on a train. Who's sick, stranger?"

Vince Attinger's footfalls sounded on the stoop. Then the youngster pushed through the batwings. "My Pa, Mister Regan. And he ain't just sick. He's dyin'."

"Howdy again, handsome," the girl called and

41

straightened up, smoothing the wrinkles from her plain red dress and then running her hands through her disarrayed hair.

"Then he ain't got a chance, boy," the fat Regan growled. "And around here, folks bury their own dead. Hey, where the hell you think you're goin'?"

His voice got loud and angry as he saw Edge heading for the open end of the bar counter. And when the half-breed swung through the gap, the fat man reached under the bartop.

"Hold it, Mister Regan!" Vince snarled, and the man froze after snapping his head around to see that the youngster had drawn his Remington revolver.

"Any charge for water in this place?" Edge asked, reaching for a bucket under the bar.

Reagan grinned cynically with his sullen lips. "Not when it's that dirty, stranger. I use that for swabbin' down the floor. That's got spit and dirt and like that in it."

"Just so long as it's wet," the half-breed said as he lifted the bucket and in three strides reached the table where McArthur was slumped.

"Put up the gun, boy," Regan said and vented a harsh laugh. "I wouldn't do anythin' in the world to stop seein' this."

"The Doc . . ." the girl started, paused until the bucket of filthy water was thrown over the sleeping drunk, and completed: ". . . won't take kindly to that."

Her warning was superfluous because before she had finished giving it, McArthur had returned to enraged awareness. He jerked upright in his chair which would have tipped over backward with the force of the move had the wall not halted it.

"You sonofabitch!" he shrieked as his derby flew off and he shook his head violently, focusing his bloodshot eyes on Edge and standing erect. His knees caught the underside of the table and tipped it over. "You sonofabitchin' bastard!"

He hurled away the shot glass, but retained his grip on the neck of the bottle as he brought it down on the rim of the overturned table. Glass shattered and he tried to lunge at the half-breed with the oldest of barroom brawling weapons—but his brain was dulled by liquor and his physical responses were slowed.

Edge had discarded the empty bucket the moment McArthur began to fold up from the table. He had the Winchester in a two-handed grip before the man started to his feet. Now he brought the barrel down hard on the wrist of the hand holding the broken bottle. The roar of anger became one of pain as the whole length of his arm was numbed and his fingers opened.

More glass shattered under one of Edge's boots as he stepped up close to McArthur and kicked the table away with a backheel move. He was holding the rifle high now, around the barrel and narrowest section of the stock. And when he leaned forward to a man almost as tall as himself, the frame of the Winchester was pressed against McArthur's throat. Then, part of a second later, the man's shoulders and the back of his head were hard to the wall—and the rifle frame threatened to burst open the skin which contoured his Adam's apple.

"Understand you're what passes for a doctor in this town?" Edge said evenly as the tall and skinny McArthur tried to counterattack with his hands—but suddenly dropped his arms to his sides

43

when the half-breed applied more pressure to the rifle. Then he eased up a little so the man was able to vent a moan that gave voice to the agonized expression on his hollow-cheeked, sunken-eyed face. "Nod or shake your head, Gerry."

McArthur, staring hatefully at his attacker, nodded. He tried to speak, but the pressure of the rifle against his throat made nonsense of the words.

"Feller on the back of a wagon outside has got a deep stab wound. Happened some time ago and he had a rough ride to get here. If we had gone through the strong, hot coffee routine to sober you, he could have died. Obliged if you'd take a look at him."

Now Edge stepped back from the dripping man, and canted the Winchester to his shoulder. He spared a glance for Regan and the girl and saw they were still shocked by what had happened and expected more trouble.

McArthur, who was in his mid-forties and dressed in an old, creased, patched and stained city suit of uncertain color massaged his punished throat with both bony hands and continued to stare his hatred at the half-breed.

Edge jerked a crooked thumb toward Vince who still had the Remington drawn and held loosely, the muzzle aimed at the floor in front of him. "That's the hurt man's son. Maybe you know another member of the family? Name of Aristotle Attinger. Lot of money there. Can afford to pay well for good service."

"You have to be as crazy as you act, mister, if you're counting on me to help you. After the way you just—"

"You've got it wrong, feller," Edge cut in. "It's not me needs the help."

44

"Please, Doc!" Vince begged. "My Pa's hurt real bad and—"

McArthur shook his head and came away from the wall, picking his way carefully over the shattered glass and between the overturned furniture. "I'm not a doctor, son," he growled, running his hands through his hair and scattering droplets of dirty water. "Just a vet who's read a few medical books. I'm not qualified to treat a man as badly injured as you say your father is." He reached the bar and said, "Give me a shot of rye, Pat."

Regan swung to lift a bottle down from a shelf, but froze when Vince Attinger fired his revolver, blasting the bullet into the floor, not close to anybody.

"Look at him, won't you?" the youngster demanded desperately as all eyes swung to look at him. "He got stuck deep with a knife and he's been out ever since. Bleedin' awful bad. You gotta have somethin' to keep the poison from startin'. And you gotta know how to stop the bleedin'!"

"Least you can do is look at the guy, Gerry," Regan said.

"I think so, too, Doc," the girl agreed.

McArthur glowered at Edge, and the other three people in the saloon expressed similar feelings but to a lesser degree than the impassive halfbreed.

"I wouldn't have done what he did," Vince added quickly.

Then McArthur swung away from the bar. "All right, son. I'll see what I can do for your father. But my fee will take account of the treatment I received at the hands of your friend."

Vince holstered his gun and began to blurt effusive thanks as he led the way out of the saloon.

45

"Seems that soaking went to his head," Edge muttered as the batwings flapped behind McArthur.

"With a friend like you, nobody needs enemies," Regan growled. And he started to return the bottle of liquor to the shelf.

"I'll take a shot of that, feller," Edge told him as he bellied up to the bar.

A glass was produced and filled to the brim. Edge paid and started to sip the whiskey.

"That all you want, mister?" the girl asked, trying not too hard to resume the come-hither attitude of a member of the oldest profession open for business.

"No."

Outside, the wagon rolled forward and the sound of its slow progress receded. Inside, the young whore advanced along the bar toward the half-breed.

"Her name's Millicent, stranger. I charge a dollar for the room. What she gets is between the two of you."

Edge finished the liquor at a swallow and eyed the young whore bleakly, halting her four feet away from him. "Like for at least this much space to be between us, Millicent," he said evenly and the professional smile froze on her dissipated features. It transformed into a scowl.

"So what else is it you want?" Regan asked sourly.

"My horse back. Old man Attinger stole him and rode in this direction. You see anything of him? A couple of hours ago, maybe?"

Regan was committed to the spit before he realized the slop bucket was no longer in its accustomed place under the bar counter. "That sick in the head old man ain't been to town in more than a month."

46

Millicent vented one of her hard to raise laughs. Regan growled. "What's so funny, girl?"

"Don't you think it's a barrel of laughs, Pat?" she answered. "That crazy old buzzard stealin' the horse of this mean hearted sonofabitch?"

"Take care, girl," Regan warned. "Or could be the stranger will get in some practice on you for what he plans to do with Attinger when he catches up with him."

"That kind of practice I don't need, feller," Edge said. "Obliged for the information."

He turned away from the bar.

"Hey, stay and have one on the house," Regan said quickly.

"You don't owe me a thing."

"It's worth a drink to hear about what happened down at that crazy old coot's place, stranger."

"And about how rich he is, mister," the girl added cynically with a pointed glance at the bartender. "Seein' as how Regan and everyone else hereabouts figured the old man broke himself buildin' that stupid boat in the desert."

At the batwings, Edge turned and looked scornfully back at the weary bartender and the young wreck of a whore amid the squalid surroundings of the malodorous saloon.

"I'm curious is all," Regan said defensively.

"No you ain't, feller," the half-breed countered. "If money didn't interest you, then you'd be an oddity."

"Close mouthed sonofabitch, ain't you?" Millicent challenged sourly.

"Maybe because it's true what they say about money talking."

"I don't get you," she sneered.

47

He nodded. "Not in word or deed, lady. On account of I've got a bad case of laryngitis."

"I know how you friggin' feel!" Gerry McArthur yelled.

And blasted a shot toward the half-breed.

Meanwhile, the doctor was in the middle of the street, his tall and gaunt frame casting a long shadow from the lamp out front of the railroad depot. And it was this moving shadow that Edge saw as he made to push open the batwings—just part of a second before McArthur began to shout. Edge recognized the distorted shape of a revolver jutting from the elongated hand and arm.

Thus, he was going backward and starting to the side before McArthur was through with words and squeezing the trigger—which saved his life. For with luck or skill the man placed his shot just above the centre of the batwings—only a fraction of time after Edge had powered from the line of fire.

Regan roared an obscenity and the girl shrieked her fear as the bullet hit a bottle on the shelf behind the bar to scatter glass fragments and liquor to the floor.

But before the sound of falling shards had ended and McArthur had the chance to thumb back on the hammer of his gun, the half-breed had resumed his place on the threshold, cocking the Winchester as part of the same action as bringing it down from his shoulder.

His ice-blue eyes were narrowed to glittering slits and his thin lips were curled back to display his white teeth in a brutal killer's grin.

He brought up a knee to part the doors and the rifle was leveled from the hip between them.

McArthur expressed a moment's rage that he

48

had missed with his first shot. Then his thin face was taken over by a frozen look of fear as he realized there was no opportunity for a second attempt.

The Winchester exploded and there was hardly a movement from the rifle or the man holding it, as the recoil was absorbed. The muzzle flash was bright. The gunsmoke was acrid in the clean, cool air.

The man at the center of the street took the bullet in his chest, left of center. He staggered backward for several steps, his arms stretched far out to the sides. Then the gun slipped from his nerveless fingers and his expression altered a final time, showing a mournful look—like he was grieving ahead of time about his own death. He glanced down at the blossoming stain on the front of his suit jacket and never looked up again. Dropping his arms to his sides, he started to fall stiffly forward, but then became limp and crumpled into an untidy heap.

"You kill him?" Regan asked hoarsely.

"Seemed like a better idea than letting him kill me, feller," Edge muttered as he went out on to the decaying stoop.

"If we took a vote on that, you'd maybe lose, mister!" Millicent snarled as she reached the batwings, hooked a hand over them to stop them swinging and glared out at the half-breed.

"We already did, lady. On a show of arms, he lost."

He didn't look back at her as he moved along the street toward the tent in front of which the flatbed wagon was parked. Inside this tent, a lamp was dimly alight. Elsewhere in Ventura, if the exchange of shots had created any interest, the occupants of the tents peered out at the tall, lean half-breed without putting matches to their lamps. Then, as he drew closer to the wagon, his footfalls disturbing the silence of the night, he became counterpointed by the wracking sobs of a man weeping.

But the sound of his approach penetrated through into Vince Attinger's private world of sorrow and the boy crawled out of the tent and had fisted the tears, but not the redness from his eyes by the time Edge reached him.

The half-breed handed back the Remington to its owner.

"Dear God, I didn't know . . ." Vince started, taking the gun before he looked down at his empty holster. Then he leaned to the side to peer around Edge to see Regan and the girl stooped over the inert form of McArthur.

"If I thought you had, kid," the half-breed said flatly, "you'd be as dead as I figure your Pa to be."

The boy slid the gun back in the holster and nodded. "Yeah, when we got him inside and started to uncover the wound, the doc saw he was gone." He showed embarrassment and looked away from the steady gaze of Edge. "I just broke up, mister. That must have been when that guy took my gun." He recovered and looked directly back at the half-breed. "I want to thank you for tryin'. For bringin' Pa to town. Now he's dead, though, nothin's changed. Except that even more I want that crazy sonofabitch found. And the money ain't the most important thing no more."

Edge nodded and climbed up on to the wagon seat, asking, "You coming?"

"Where?"

50

"The old-timer wasn't through here tonight. But he won't be far away. In case it rains."

Vince shook his head. "No. I can't do anythin' until tomorrow but I want to see that Pa has a proper burial."

"Suit yourself."

The boy reached out a hand to hold the bridle of one of the team horses. "If you find him, mister . . . ? You'll let me know? You won't just . . . ?"

"Depends where he is and you are, kid," Edge answered. "Matter of a stolen horse to be settled first thing. After that, maybe we can do business on that finder's fee."

Vince nodded morosely and let go of the bridle. "Reckon that'll have to be good enough."

Edge released the brake, clucked to the horses and steered them into a tight turn across the width of the street, sensing the distrust in the eyes of the boy as they gazed at his back.

As the wagon rolled slowly southward, Millicent emerged from the saloon after helping Regan to carry the corpse of McArthur inside. She held up a hand and hurried to the side of the wagon when the half-breed reined in the team.

"Mister," she said in a hoarse whisper, and shot a nervous glance over her shoulder toward the batwings. "I want to ask a favor."

"Only give them in exchange, lady. And yours don't appeal to me."

She was petulantly impatient, then showed anger when another glance over her shoulder revealed Pat Regan standing on the threshold of the saloon. "Damn him," she rasped, and raised her voice to snarl up at the half-breed. "Now that you killed the doc, reckon I'll see if I can be of any help to the injured man!"

"He ain't just injured any more," Edge answered. "If you want to help his son, take a shovel."

She tossed her head. "Then I'll comfort the livin'."

"Why not?" Edge murmured as the whore swung away to head along the street. "He's already gone to pieces. Maybe do him good. Having a piece go to him."

swered. "If you want to help his son, pack
should.

She tossed her head. "Then I'll come if
to."

Why not?" he said and nodded. "Then

Chapter Five

WITHOUT the need to consider a dying man in
the back, Edge made better time on the return
trip to the ark and shack of Telly Attinger. But he
did not push the team too hard. Primarily because
there was no urgency and also because, he was
forced to admit to himself, he was not anxious to
find what he expected at the end of the south
bound trail.

And he was still more than a quarter of a mile
from his destination when he saw the first sign
that his suspicion was well founded. For in the
bright light of the moon he saw just two horses in
the corral out back of the darkened shack. When
he had left there had been the mounts of Augie
and Vince plus Crystal Dickens's stallion. After he
halted the wagon, he saw it was the woman's
horse which was missing.

Still not hurrying, and with a set expression of
indifference carved across his features, he took
the team from the traces and turned them loose in
the corral. Then he went in through the open
doorway of the shack and struck a match, intend-
ing to light the kerosene lamp. But in the initial

flare and then in the flickering light of the flame, he saw as much as he needed.

The place had been wrecked by the process of a frantic search which had not ended until a desperate clawing at the dirt floor had uncovered a metal-lined hole in the ground to the left of the now cold stove. The lid which had rested over the hole, once covered with stamped down earth, had been flung across the room in the exhilaration of the find. And the lamp on the floor beside the hole had been left burning in the haste to escape: it was now empty of oil.

Edge allowed himself just a short grunt of mild displeasure as he blew out the match flame an instant before it would have burned his thumb and finger. Then he backed from the shack and went around to the rear without glancing at the massive ark held upright in the cradle of timber.

He got his saddle and bedroll from the wagon and elected to use the all-black gelding of Augie Attinger rather than Vince's pinto. But the color did not influence his selection, which was based solely upon the fact that Augie was dead.

Then he led the horse on a slow circuit of the shack and ark, swinging wide so as not to be confused by the surfeit of signs in the immediate area. He did not climb into the saddle until he was certain of the direction in which the woman had ridden. A little to the east of north, starting out from beside were two elongated indentations in the earth just beyond the corral fence. They were grave size, but with the ground concave instead of convex.

And not for the first time, the slow riding half-breed recalled something the old-timer had yelled when he was on his knees between his son and grandson after the boy exploded his gun. *No other folks must die on account of what I been told to do by the good Lord.* And, before that, when he was forced to admit he doctored the food, *I wouldn't knowingly harm any living creature.*

No other and *knowingly* were the key words which could well mean that two strangers passing through earlier to the shack of the crazy old man had failed to realize anything was wrong with the food Telly Attinger cooked up for them.

But, as before when he considered these out-of-context snatches of fervid rantings by the religious fanatic, Edge wasted little time reflecting upon them—because the words and their implications were no concern of his. And on this occasion he turned his thoughts to the brown-eyed, dark blonde woman from New England via New York City, and tried with total lack of success to feel contempt toward her for what she had done and was doing.

The high wind at the start of the night had smoothed the terrain and obliterated whatever sign was impressed into the dust before the storm. And with the bright moon low in the sky, casting clearly delineated shadows, it required little concentrated effort for the half-breed to stay on the hooftracks left by Crystal Dickens's horse—particularly after he realized the woman had her sights fixed on an outcrop of rock which jutted up into the sky like a shortened finger from among the ridges to the east of Ventura.

And he allowed himself a quiet smile with his lips when he discovered this. For he had taught her the importance of taking a bearing on some distant feature of the landscape when riding across flatlands. This on the long ride from Irving Texas to Telly Attinger's folly.

What else had he taught her? Back in the small Texas town, during the long days and nights on the trail, and at the crazy old-timer's shack? That she was doing the wrong thing in hooking up with him. He had made that plain from the very outset and then he never missed any opportunity to reemphasize his opinion—by hurting her pride or causing her physical pain.

But never had he come straight out and told her he did not want her with him. For that would have been a lie. And despite the kind of man he had become after he found the mutilated corpse of his brother at the Iowa farm, he still retained a fingerhold on a pitifully few of the finer human virtues. Truth was one of these.

Occasionally he allowed himself to bend his set of personal rules: as when, riding on the wagon with Vince and the dying Augie, he had claimed to be happy with his own thoughts. He was far from content then, while he considered Crystal's motives for remaining at old man Attinger's shack. And suspecting the worst of her.

And now he knew he was right to doubt her. Had seen for himself undeniable evidence of her guile and cunning. She had never intended to wait for the old-timer to return—and certainly her decision to stay behind while the wounded man was taken to Ventura formed no part of any test to see if the half-breed would come back for her.

The desire for easy money was her sole reason. For, like Edge, she had heard Telly Attinger make a point of warning them his cache was not hidden in the shack. And she had figured out that, because the old man spoke unbidden in these terms, there was a good chance he lied. Added to this was the thought that a man with a great deal of money to protect was likely to store it close to him. And until his vision came true and the flood swept across southeastern Utah, the shack was a safer place than the ark.

The secret compartment in the galley of the boat? In periods of sanity between religious fervor, maybe Attinger figured there would still be value in money after the waters receded.

The half-breed spat into the dust and took out the makings from a shirt pocket as he abandoned this line of thought. It was entirely theoretical and virtually never ending in the way it demanded more guesses concerning why Aristotle Attinger stabbed his son and rode off into the night because of the discovery of an empty hole in the floor.

He abandoned it because the money and the trouble it had caused in the Attinger family was of scant interest to him.

Crystal Dickens was—and had been ever since he first saw her—in the Red Dog Saloon back at Irving. But he had endured an inner struggle to deny the attraction he felt toward her and had succeeded during the entire time they were together. He needed her, but knew from his harsh experiences of the past that to admit this was to declare open house to pain and suffering. For the woman and for himself.

He struck a match on the rifle stock and touched the flame to the end of the newly rolled cigarette. And in the flare, the slivers of ice blue eyes between the almost closed lids expressed to the empty night a powerful mixture of anguish and hatred.

He tossed the match away and a tremor shook his hand.

The gelding under him snorted.

"It appears I'm real cold, feller," the half-breed said softly, stroking the animal's neck and halting him for a few moments while he took his top coat from the bedroll and donned it. He turned up the collar so that it brushed the underside of his hatbrim around his ears and at the nape of his neck.

He clucked his mount forward again.

It was crazy.

He felt a great attraction to and need for the woman. And she had been willing to fulfil his desires. But to accept what she offered was to invite yet another cruel twist of his ruling fate—and to protect both of them from this, he had shown her only the worst sides of what he was.

Since they were both suffering anyway how could he blame her for what she had done? A green girl from Vermont who had come west in search of a man and found him. A man who had taught her much more than how to ride across deserts and through mountains without going around in circles. Who had, by example, taught her that the world in which he existed was a hard one, and his design for staying alive in it was to beat it at its own game—and to hell with the consequences.

That had been his code for a long time. So why had he put her to the test by allowing her to remain at the old man's shack? And why, after she had taken a course of independent action which owed much to what she had learned from him, was he tracking her?

It had to be because, in this case, the consequences did matter.

He told himself he was riding through the Utah night because all the evidence pointed to Crystal Dickens being a thief.

And after this he gave up searching his mind for answers as he continued to scan the country on all sides in his habitual attitude of vigilence from behind a shield of apparent indifference to his surroundings.

The eastern horizon was lightening in advance of dawn by the time he rode off the flatland and into the hills. And as he rested himself and his horse while he sat on a rock and ate a breakfast of jerked beef washed down with water from his canteen, the sun came up. It was completely clear of the horizon, bright, yellow and pleasantly warm when he climbed into the saddle again, his coat back in the bedroll.

The sign was more difficult to see now, because of the daylight and the hardness of the higher ground which was less susceptible to retaining impressions of hooves. But the tall, lean, long-haired half-breed was skilled in the art of tracking and he made good time through gulleys, along arroyos and across slopes. Only occasionally did he dismount and lead the horse by the reins to ensure he did not miss some vital sign that the woman had swung on to a different course.

The column of rock which had been her marker toward the hills was now behind him and after awhile he knew that a flat topped rise with a niche cut into its rim had become her new destination. And her course continued to lay northeast: She veered to left or right only when the way directly ahead was obstructed by an escarpment, steep drop, or ravine.

Above the mesa-like rise and as far as the eye

could see to either side of it, a bank of dark cloud was building up—but very slowly. To the south, east, and west the sky was a brilliant blue. The sun's heat and glare reached a greater intensity with each minute that elapsed and the shade temperature seemed to be no different than that in the dazzling light.

Edge drank sparingly from his canteen and also rationed the gelding to just an occasional few drops of water offered in his cupped hands.

He sweated a great deal and was constantly aware of the discomfort of sprouting bristles on his lower face. He was conscious, too, of the gritty sensation under his eyelids from lack of sleep. But the rigors of life on the trail were nothing new to a drifter such as Edge. And on the hot morning of this Utah day he paid even less attention than usual to the ordeal. For he knew that if disaster hit—if his food and water were taken from him somehow or the gelding went lame—then the tent town of Ventura was within easy reach to the southwest.

But at mid-morning the signs of another source of danger showed: the portents of a threat—an assumed threat—that caused the half-breed to draw back his lips and crack his eyes to the narrowest of glinting slits as he reined in the gelding and swung down from the saddle.

It was at a point where two natural trails through the hills came together under a triangular shaped crag—one from the northeast and the other from the northwest. Crystal Dickens had rested here. Lit a fire and drank some coffee. Eaten a can of beans. Urinated. Had kicked off her boots and walked around bare footed for awhile.

All the signs were there to be read.

And they had been seen and interpreted by eyes other than those of the half-breed: three riders who had been heading down the trail from the northwest. Two heavily built men and one of average size. A cigar smoker in the trio—maybe the same one who spit a great deal. They had come upon the campsite after the woman left to continue on her northeastward way. How long afterwards and the period of time they had spent there was impossible to judge.

What could be seen was that they had remounted their horses and taken off in the wake of Crystal Dickens.

Edge remained under the crag for less than a minute, staying astride his gelding. Then he took the same route.

With the sign of four horses to follow, the tracking chore was much easier. The half-breed resisted the temptation to demand a faster pace from his mount in the blistering heat. But it was not simply the risk of exhausting the gelding that caused him to keep his progress cautious. Greater speed meant more noise and he was wary of announcing his presence on the back trail of the trio following the woman.

And when he discovered, at high noon, that he need not have been concerned about anyone hearing his approach, he did not consider his caution as wasted effort. Countless times in the past he had escaped death by being on his guard against a menace when there was no rational reason to expect one.

He rode out of the mouth of a gully and halted his horse at the top of a man-made embankment to look down a shallow incline at the sun glinting tracks of a railroad curving around the base of a hill which had been blasted and cut away to improve the grade for the line.

To the southwest the rails and ties were featureless. Crystal Dickens was lying across the track to the northeast, perhaps a hundred yards away from where Edge dismounted and led the gelding carefully down the slope.

The woman heard the shod hooves striking the smooth rock and wrenched her head to the side to peer toward the source of the sound.

"Edge?" she shouted, her voice hoarse and her tone making the name into a query.

He did not reply. He reached the foot of the embankment and led his horse at an easy walk alongside the track which was laid upon a two feet high bed of crushed rock.

"Edge?" Crystal shouted again, and sobbed. "Answer me, please! Is it really you?"

"Been told there ain't nobody like me, lady," the half-breed said now. "So I guess it has to be."

"Thank God! Oh, my dear God! Thank you!"

When he was level with her, he left his horse and stepped up on to the track and saw why she had not been certain who he was.

They had tied her ankles together and her wrists behind her back. Then roped her knees and her neck to the rails several hours ago. Long enough for the searing sun to raise blisters on her face which she could turn to left and right but never achieve shade for all of it at one time. So that no part of her facial flesh had escaped the punishment of exposure to sunburn—including her eyelids which were raw and inflamed, all but blinding her. Apart from her hat which was beside the track, she was fully dressed and there was no sign that they had done anything to her except leave her to fry or be cut into three by a locomotive.

He dropped to his haunches beside her, tipped a little water from a canteen into his cupped hand and trickled it on to her swollen lips.

"More," she croaked after her tongue had come out to taste the water.

"Later," he answered.

"Please."

"Shut up!" he snapped.

She forced open her eyes wider than they wanted and grimaced at the pain it caused. "You have a right to be mad at me, but can't you wait until—?"

"Shut up and listen!" he ordered. Then went down on his hands and knees and pressed an ear to a rail, grunting when he felt the vibration backing up the humming sound.

The woman screwed her head around to stare at him and despite the sun-punished ugliness of her face, her features clearly showed terror.

"Is it. . . . ?" she started. And gasped to signal that she could now feel the trembling of the rails.

"Figure you don't need me to lay it on the line for you?" he said as he got back up on to his haunches and glanced along the railroad as he drew the razor from the neck pouch.

He could see only two hundred yards of track before it curved out of sight beyond the start of the man-made cutting through the hills. But neither he nor the woman needed to see the approaching train. It was close enough now for the thud of the locomotive's pistons to mask the humming of the rails.

"Hurry, hurry!" Crystal Dickens screamed.

Edge worked fast but not frenetically, first sawing through the rope which held her neck, and then slicing through the bonds at her knees.

"I can't move, I can't move!" she shrieked, the blisters on her lips bursting to leak their liquid contents as she forced her mouth wide.

The half-breed did not hear her panic because the thunderous sounds of the approaching train filled his ears as the locomotive raced into the curving cutting. But he did not need to hear her words: He knew that after being held a prisoner in one posture for so long, it was unlikely that she would be able to move a muscle.

He threw himself off the track with the train whistle blasting out to mask every sound except for the scream of locked wheels sliding along rails. Certainly the strident warning of the whistle covered the scream of the woman as he hooked his hands under her armpits and wrenched her clear of the locomotive's skidding wheels. A scream of agony triggered from every nerve ending in her body as her every fibre protested the sudden jerking from inertia.

Then she was silent and limp in merciful unconsciousness. And Edge felt pain from the jetting steam that hissed from valves and billowed over the woman and himself as they sprawled along the side of the track bed, only inches from the spark-showering wheels.

Time played tricks as Edge lay between the unfeeling woman and the track, shielding her from scalding steam and searing sparks, so that it seemed to take an incredibly long sequence of seconds, minutes, and even hours before the ground ceased to tremble, the clatter of wheels was curtailed, and the halted locomotive began to vent a steady hissing sound—almost gentle in contrast to the cacophony of the train's emergency stop.

Then Edge heard the beat of hooves on rock and raised his head in time to see the black gelding gallop out of sight around the curve of rock from which the train had appeared. Next he heard men's voices, harsh with anger and shrill with anxiety.

It was the brakeman who was snarling obscene demands for an explanation as he climbed down from the caboose some forty yards away from where Edge eased painfully up on to his haunches. The engineer and fireman also worried, ran along the side of the line of stalled freight cars.

The half-breed rolled Crystal Dickens gently over on to her back before he straightened up to his full height and turned to face the thin, short, somewhere around fifty-year-old brakeman who was first to reach him.

"What the frig you people think you're a doin'?" the railroadman snarled breathlessly. "You could've caused a wreck, you know that?"

Edge, his lips curled back from his teeth and slitted eyes glinting dangerously, reached out one hand toward the man. Bunching the lapels of his worse for wear uniform jacket together, lifted him clear of the ground, swinging into a half turn and slamming him hard against the side of a car. The slightly built man was dumbstruck when he realized the extent of Edge's strength and the power of the emotion seething in him. Then he was forced to vent a cry of pain as his spine and the back of his head impacted with the car side.

"Hey, you! What's Charlie done to you?"

The engineer was in the same age group as the brakeman and looked just as scared as he stopped short. It was the much younger, coal and oil stained fireman who snarled the words when he skidded to a breathless halt much closer to where the woman lay and the half-breed held the man a prisoner against the car.

Edge squeezed his eyes closed and allowed the dangerous layer of his rage to rasp out in a sigh. Then said, as he set Charlie down on his feet and released him, "He riled me, feller."

"The lady?" the engineer asked and took a few nervous steps forward. "Is she hurt?"

"Figure when she wakes up she'll decide there were times when she felt better."

"What in hell happened?" the fireman wanted to know, grimacing down at the woman's sun-punished face.

"That's all I friggin' asked," the brakeman growled as he smoothed down the crumpled lapels of his ancient uniform jacket. "There was no call for him to do what he done to me!"

"Like for you fellers to get her aboard the caboose, out of the sun," Edge said.

"Sure. Sure, we'll do that." The engineer was eager to help, obviously afraid the brakeman was in danger of arousing the half-breed's anger again. "We'll roll into Ventura in less than thirty minutes, mister. There's a kinda doctor there named McArthur. He'll know what to do for what ails the lady."

Edge turned away from the group of railroadmen without enlightening the engineer about the fate of Gerry McArthur.

"Hey, where you goin'?" the young fireman demanded.

66

"Get my horse."

"Ain't you gonna ride in on the train?"

"Like for you to wait."

"Frig that!" Charlie snapped, and dug a watch from his vest pocket. "You already put us behind schedule. Anyways we don't handle livestock—or passengers for that matter, in the normal run of things."

"Keep your hair on, Charlie," the engineer placated and nodded to Edge who had halted to look back over his shoulder. "We'll wait a few minutes, mister. Then we gotta pull out to pick up a load of ore which is all we usually carry."

The half-breed spat at a car wheel and the globule of saliva dried almost at once on the hot metal. "If you fellers leave before I get back, you should know about something I carry."

"What the frig you talkin' about?" the testy brakeman wanted to know.

Edge pursed his lips and rasped curtly: "Grudges."

Chapter Six

IT took Edge ten minutes to find the still nervous black gelding, capture him and bring him back to the stalled train. While the irritable brakeman helped to coax the horse aboard a freight car, the fireman was working to keep up steam pressure in the locomotive's boiler, and the engineer sat beside the comatose woman in the caboose.

"We can pull out now?" Charlie asked with heavy sarcasm as Edge unsaddled the horse.

"No sweat, feller."

The brakeman climbed off the car and stooped to raise the sidegate, asking, "Well, ain't you friggin' comin'?"

"This horse don't like trains," Edge answered as he took out the makings. "I'll ride with him."

Fear encroached on Charlie's testiness. "But what if somethin' happens to that woman?"

"If she wakes up and asks where I am, you tell her, feller."

"She could die on me."

Edge ran his tongue along the gummed strip of paper and finished rolling the cigarette. "If it's extra to haul dead weight, I'll pay."

He struck a match as Charlie slammed up the

68

gate and fixed it in position. Moments later he was in the caboose and the engineer was climbing down.

"She's breathin' easier now she's in the shade, mister," the railroadman reported. "I sure hope that quack in Ventura has somethin' to take the heat outta those burns on her face."

"He ain't around any more, feller."

"McArthur's left town?"

"Body and soul. He's left everywhere."

The engineer gulped. "You mean he's—"

"Maybe has just a ghost of a chance of returning."

The man shook his head in dismay and started to trudge morosely along the line of cars toward the hissing and smoking locomotive, muttering, "Whatever is this world comin' to?"

Edge glanced northward, to where the bank of clouds had thickened and darkened, but had not encroached any further across the otherwise blue sky. "Figure awhile yet before the end," he murmured.

The engineer clambered up on to the locomotive footplate and the half-breed braced himself in a corner of the car. His cigarette slanted from a side of his mouth while he held the gelding's bridle in one hand and stroked the animal's neck with the other. Then began to talk softly to the horse whose ears were pricked and nostrils flared.

The locomotive inched forward and the line of cars clanked into each other as they were jerked into movement. The horse snorted, curled his upper lip and trembled.

"Easy, feller, easy," Edge drawled, needing all his strength to hold the bridle and keep the animal from tossing his head, maybe as a signal that he was about to rear. "All right, all right. It's a lot better than me riding you. One, two three . . . Monday, Tuesday, Wednesday . . . January, February, March . . ."

By the time he had counted slowly to ten, ran through the days of the week and half the months of the year, the train was moving steadily, the clack of rolling wheels sounding in a regular cadence. And the gelding was calm, maybe relishing as much as the half-breed the cooling effect of the slipstream. Then it was necessary only every now and again to stroke the animal's neck and murmur more words close to a pricked ear—when the car jolted on one of the curves.

Less occasionally, after the cigarette had gone out but remained slanted from his lips, Edge glanced over his shoulder toward the caboose which was immediately behind the car. But if there was any change for better or worse in Crystal's condition, Charlie made no attempt to signal it.

But for most of the time the half-breed maintained a narrow-eyed survey over the country to either side of the track, searching the rocky terrain for three riders. And failing.

Then the locomotive was throttled back more than usual as another curve showed ahead. It did not pick up speed on the straightaway, for at the end of it, was Ventura.

Little interest was shown in the slowing train by the men working the claims on which their tents were pitched. Just here and there a head was turned or a hand was raised in greeting. Smoke wisped up from dying fires on which midday meals had been cooked and on a few of the claims

70

men lingered over a last cup of coffee before returning to work.

Two people engaged in a digging chore on a lot out back of Regan's Place were not grubbing for silver bearing rock. Around them the arid earth was dotted with wooden crosses to mark the unfenced area as the local cemetery. And as the train rolled to a halt, Edge recognized the gravediggers as Vince Attinger and Millicent the young whore.

". . . . yeah, that's right, Don. He sure looks like the one Pat told me gunned down Gerry McArthur."

Edge looked toward the railroad depot building and saw a small, rotund, bald-headed man in a neat uniform emerge from the shade of the awning, flanked by the engineer and the fireman. He went toward the caboose as Charlie yelled:

"She don't look no better nor no worse, mister."

The half-breed nodded and answered, "Obliged." Then cinched his saddle to the gelding and lashed his bedroll to the back.

He guessed he wasn't supposed to hear the engineer's warning to the depot manager: "Be careful, Mr. Crane. He riles easy."

He was working to loosen the fastenings on the sidegate when the smartly uniformed man came to a halt and demanded:

"What's this about a woman on the line and you dragging her clear, sir?"

"There was one and I did it, feller," Edge supplied. "Like for you to lower this gate gently. This horse is spooked by loud noises."

"That's not good enough, sir," the manager countered. "I have to put in a report to head office about incidents on the line. With full details."

71

The engineer moved hurriedly forward to comply with Edge's request and then all the railroadmen backed off when the gelding got skittish as he was encouraged down off the car. Then, when the horse felt firm ground beneath his hooves, he was docile again.

"Sir," the manager called when Edge began to lead the animal toward the caboose. "Please, sir. We all have our jobs to do."

The half-breed hitched the reins to the guard rail on the rear platform of the caboose and climbed up the steps and halted to look toward the anxious man in the uniform. He nodded and replied, "That's right, feller. Or to put it another way, we all have our business to mind."

Inside the caboose, Charlie had done what he could to make the woman comfortable—had taken both cushions off his swivel chair and placed them under her head, then moved a couple of heavy crates to wedge her against the side and prevent her from rolling around.

Edge shifted the crates, got both arms under her and lifted her, draping her limp form gently over a shoulder to carry her out on to the platform and down the steps.

"She's not—" the engineer started anxiously.

"She's hot as hell, but she ain't gone there yet," the half-breed answered. "What do I owe for the ride?"

"A horse and two passengers from Colorado Junction would cost—" the manager said.

"No charge," the engineer cut in and received an angry glare from the uniformed man. He ignored it and explained, "It was a mercy mission."

"Obliged, feller," Edge responded and with his free hand unhitched the reins from the guardrail.

"Surprised you understand what Don's talking about, sir," Crane growled. "Way I hear it, you didn't understand the meaning of mercy when you shot down Gerald McArthur."

"Words I understand," Edge answered without turning around as he moved away from the rear of the train. "It's people that sometimes puzzle me."

Crane vented a grunt of scorn. "I've met your type before!" he called after the departing half-breed. "What you fail to understand, you destroy!"

Now Edge did look back as he led his horse over the railroad track and answered; "Take the engineer's advice, feller. Watch what you say or there could be a question mark over your future."

There was a babble of talk behind him, Crane speaking angrily while the train crew tried to placate him. But none of it was loud enough to be heard by Edge as he moved with the unconscious woman and the horse along the street. He was heading for the tent of the dead McArthur and by the time he reached it there were signs of increased activity out on the claims. The silver miners loading heavy looking sacks on to handcarts which when fully laden, were trundled down to the trail and along it toward the newly arrived train.

He and Crystal Dickens were inside the tent before the first of the carts was pushed past the closed entrance flap. It was a three man wedge tent of a design the half-breed had seen often in army camps during the War between the States. Reasonably cool in the heat of early afternoon, the canvas subdued the glaring light of the sun to a restful shade of green.

Along one side was an unfurled bedroll on a

short legged cot, the blanket stained with the spilled blood of Augie Attinger. Across from this was a Boston rocker chair, a four drawer chest without legs, two wooden crates containing a supply of canned and jarred foods and cooking and eating utensils, and a latrine pail that was empty. There was a thin pitcher and basin on the chest and a Paul Revere candle lamp hanging from the underside of the tent ridge.

Edge arranged the woman in what seemed to be the most comfortable posture on the cot and covered her with McArthur's blankets and those from his own bedroll. Then he looked through the drawers of the chest. The lower two contained clothing and the others were untidy with jars, bottles, cans and earthenware tubs of medicaments mixed in with a selection of tarnished surgical instruments. None of the containers were labeled and Edge opened several before he found a likely looking white salve.

It smelled and felt right, but first he tested it on himself—used the razor from the neck pouch to make a small cut on the ball of his thumb and spread a little of the ointment on it. After a few seconds, when he failed to feel any sting, he spread the salve thinly over the disfigured face of the unconscious woman.

In the cool and restful light of the tent, tiredness threatened to catch up with him. So before making any attempt to rouse Crystal Dickens, he used the tepid water in the pitcher to wash up and shave. It still felt as if there was grit under his eyelids and his muscles seemed to be made of rubber, but it was better than before.

And now, as the to and fro traffic of the pushcarts continued outside, he squatted beside the woman and began to trickle water from a canteen into her mouth. After a few seconds she moaned softly. Then her tongue protruded in an involuntary move to secure more water for her parched throat. Her eyelids flickered but stayed closed. She sighed and seemed to be sinking back into a deep sleep rather than unconsciousness.

"Come on, lady," he growled, and tried a shock treatment—forcing open her lips with a thumb and finger and pouring about a quarter of a cupful of water between them.

Some of it went into her windpipe instead of her gullet and she choked, gagged and then groaned. Her head was wrenched to the side and her eyes snapped open, glazing for stretched seconds.

"Welcome back," he said softly and her eyes cleared of the film and became filled with remembered terror. "You're all in one piece, lady," he went on in the same even tone.

She had a dim recollection of hearing his voice before. Now she straightened her head on the pillow and peered directly into his face.

"Edge," she whispered at length, then shuddered from shoulders to feet. "God, I'm so cold." Then she started to lick her lips, tasted the salve and looked as if she was going to be sick.

"Easy," he said. "Just some ointment for what the sun did to your face. Too much sun will do that. Burn you up and then make you feel cold."

She shuddered again, squeezed her eyes closed and turned her head to the side. A woman in pain but instinctively aware of being a woman as she groaned, "God, I must look awful."

"Be best if you don't go near any mirrors for awhile, lady," he confirmed. "What did they get?"

"What?"

Edge sighed, rose from beside her and went to sit on the rocker. He took out the makings and began to roll a cigarette. She continued to keep her face turned toward the canvas of the tent side.

"I'm thirsty, Edge."

"Canteen right beside the bed."

"I feel bad. I need help."

"You've known me long enough, lady." He struck a match on the butt of his holstered Colt and lit the cigarette. "Favors are just a line I trade in. Way things stand right now, you owe me."

She made a sound that was like a sob and shuddered again—whether with emotion or the effects of too much sun it was impossible to tell. Time slid by and the sounds of the miners loading the train were all that disturbed the silence within the tent. They seemed to come from much further away than the railroad depot.

"Nothing," Crystal said at length. And snaked one arm out from under the blankets, the fingers splayed to explore the ground for the canteen. She found it, lifted it across her body then had to use her other hand to take out the cork.

"Not too much right away," he advised as she began to drink. Awkwardly with her head to the side, spilling more on to the pillow than she sucked down her throat.

"You went back?" she said.

"Yeah."

She sipped some water. "I didn't think you would. That's why I . . . God, I wish I'd waited, Edge." Another few drops of water from the canteen. "Those men, I thought they were going to . . . " She shuddered again and this time it was obviously triggered by remembered terror. "But they didn't . . . didn't touch me in that way. They just wanted the canteens and the food in the saddlebags and my horse. And they tied me to the railroad and waited for a train to come. But when it didn't come, they rode away. One of them, tall and very big, wanted to shoot me. But the other two said no."

Either she gulped too much water at once or the memory of fear constricted her throat. She choked and the pain caused a groan to follow it. Her voice was husky when she added; "They said that if the train didn't come through before nightfall, I'd be dead anyway. That the sun would have killed me. Bullets cost money."

"Which they didn't have, lady—even when they'd taken your horse and everything that was on him?"

Now she jerked her head over on the pillow, but the grimace of pain this brought to her unsightly, salve smeared face remained there for no longer than a second. It was replaced by an expression of indignation. "What are you saying to me? Are you accusing me of something, Edge?"

The half-breed fixed her with a glinting, narrow-eyed gaze through the layer of blue cigarette smoke that shifted lazily between them. She stared back with equal intensity and did not roll her head on the pillow and switch her attention to the roof of the tent until he started to reply.

"I told you I went back to old man Attinger's place," he said coldly. "And I didn't just take off after you when I saw your horse was gone. I checked inside the shack."

He paused and a moment before he was about

to end it, she spoke; her voice as cold and hard as his had been—but with the added ingredient of bitterness.

"Whatever you found in there has nothing to do with me. What I said to you about waiting for Mister Attinger to come back was just an excuse, Edge. I wanted to test you. To see if you'd come back for me. But after awhile I figured out I was being stupid. Ever since we met in Irving I've been just two things to you. A woman when you needed one and a burden for the rest of the time."

Now her voice cracked and the hardness and coldness was driven out by the overpowering weight of bitterness. "Dear God, when the old man's son and grandson showed up out there I even considered making up to the kid so that you'd be rid of me without feeling any guilt. Then, last night, when I was sure you wouldn't come back, I realized how much of a fool I was being. That if you didn't give a damn about me, you sure didn't feel any obligation toward me. So I just up and left. And kept off the trail because I didn't want to go to Ventura if you were still there."

Edge dropped the cigarette to the hard-packed ground and crushed out its embers beneath a boot heel. Then, when he stood up, she looked at him again. And he saw the teardrops glistening in her eyes.

"I wasn't wrong, was I?" she asked in a pained voice.

"About what, lady?"

"You wanting to be rid of me. It wasn't me you went back to the old man's place for. It was something else. But I swear to you, Edge. Whatever it was you found there and didn't like, I had nothing to do with it. All I wanted to do was to get back to where I belong. And when I found that railroad I thought I was all but there. That I could stop a train and . . . "

The words were drowned by tears and she again wrenched her head to the side to hide her face from him.

He turned and ducked to go out of the shade of the tent into the dazzlingly glare of the sun.

"Where you are going?" she asked, shrill and afraid.

"To take care of my horse."

"I don't even know where I am."

"Ventura."

He went outside and Vince Attinger came to an abrupt stop.

"I heard you and Miss Dickens came in on the train, mister. And that she was hurt."

"A little burned is all," Edge answered evenly.

The youngster remained anxious. "She's inside the tent? She doesn't need anything?"

"She's inside, kid," the half-breed confirmed. "Lying down right now. Or maybe just plain lying."

Chapter Seven

THERE was a livery stable out back of the combination saloon and store run by the grey moustached, almost bald Pat Regan. And Edge put his horse in a stall and saw to it that the animal had feed and water before he went around to the front and entered through the batwings.

The place was empty and remained so for more than a minute after the half-breed had sat at a table closest to the bar counter, his impassive face revealing no sign of the conflicting trains of thought which ran through his mind. The voices of the men loading the freight cars drifted across the street and into the saloon. From nearby came the talk between Regan and a customer in the store section of the building. The customer left with his supplies and Regan appeared through the arch in back of the bar counter. The man looked surprised to see somebody at a table—unpleasantly so when he recognized the half-breed.

"Something you want, stranger?" he asked sourly.

"Tell you I've put my horse in your livery, feller. And a beer."

"Half a buck a day for the stablin'," Regan said

as he drew the beer and placed it on the counter within reach of where Edge sat.

A dollar bill was given and change was received before Edge picked up the beer and drank half of it at a swallow.

"Owe you anything else?"

"For what?"

"You brought McArthur in here last night. I don't see him now. Or smell him."

Regan grimaced and wiped sweat off his forehead with a bare arm. "The kid who rode in with you buried his Pa and Gerry McArthur, too. Him and Millicent."

Footfalls had rapped on a stairway and now the young whore came out of the arch behind the bar. She was attired in a store bought black dress that was old but clean. And she had washed up, brushed her hair and applied fresh paint and powder to her face after her exertions in the make-shift cemetery of Ventura.

"No charge, mister," she said grimly. "I done what I could to help Vincent."

Edge acknowledged this with a nod as the girl came out from behind the bar counter and went to sit at the table where, the night before, Edge had poured the pail of dirty water over McArthur. For awhile, Regan wiped glasses and shared tacit rancor between the whore and the half-breed in equal measure. Then a bell on the store doorway jangled and he went through the archway.

Millicent stood up, approached the table where Edge sat and asked: "Can I join you, mister?"

"Long as you ain't selling. On account of I ain't buying."

She pulled out the chair opposite him and sat down. "I'm through with all that. It was never

81

supposed to be that way and I want to leave this place and forget everything I ever did here, mister."

"Telling a moving story never got anyone any place," Edge answered.

She pouted. "I ain't askin' you for anythin'."

"Then no sweat."

"Except about your friend."

"Friend?"

"Vincent."

"He say he was that?"

She pouted again, then sighed. "I just figured . . . hell, I don't know from anythin', mister. That's the trouble. He ain't said a lot. Too upset about his Pa gettin' killed, I guess. But I kinda think that if I asked him, he'd let me go with him. When he leaves Ventura."

Edge finished his beer as the bell on the store door sounded again. "It's him you should be talking to, not me," he said.

Now Millicent licked her lips and her eyes showed anxiety. "But I need to know I won't be jumpin' outta the fryin' pan into the fire, mister. After what's happened, it's plain Vincent ain't his usual self. If I ask him and he takes me, maybe when he's got over losin' his Pa he'll turn out to be a . . . " She shrugged. "Hell, I don't know."

"Think on what I told you girl," Regan growled as he came out through the archway. "Best you stay here with someone who can take care of you. That Attinger ain't nothin' but a wet-behind-the-ears kid who'll likely dump you soon as some other piece of ass that interests him shows up. Or take a powder at the first sign of trouble."

Millicent eyed the morose Regan with deepening concern, obviously mulling over again this thought which had been implanted in her mind earlier.

"Another beer," Edge asked as slow moving hoofbeats approached along the street from the north.

"Anythin' for the girl?" Regan said as he refilled the half-breed's glass.

"Advice is free and I ain't even handing out that."

Three riders halted their mounts outside, swung down from the saddles and hitched the reins to the rail.

"Sure hope these guys are bigger spenders than you are," the bartender growled as he made change for Edge and the newcomers crossed the crumbling stoop.

"Figure they've got what it takes to be," the half-breed answered evenly after glancing at the trio of strangers who came through the batwings: A man in his mid forties who was six feet tall and broadly built with muscular flesh, followed by two in their late twenties. One of them was also as tall as a grave is deep, but the thickness of his frame was due mostly to flabby fat that bulged out his clothing. The second one was medium in all things.

They were dressed Western style for riding long trails over rough terrain and unshaven and dirty from many days of not washing up. All of them packed Frontier Colts in tied down holsters, with knives in sheaths on the other hip.

There was not a trace of a smile between them as they surveyed the spartan saloon and its three occupants with red-rimmed, blood-shot eyes.

"Afternoon, strangers," Regan greeted dully. "What's your pleasure?"

"Three beers, three shot glasses and a bottle of rye," the eldest man responded as he dropped into a chair nearest the doorway and faced it, setting down a pair of saddlebags on the table at his side.

His partners slumped wearily into chairs across the table from him. The fat one rested his elbows on the table top and tried to ease his fatigue by massaging his ballooned cheeks and brightness-punished eyes. The other one gazed with arrogant insolence at Millicent, spared a glance for Edge and saw nothing that looked like a challenge in the half-breed's expression. He asked, "You with him or you available?"

The girl answered dully, "Neither."

Regan delivered a tray with the drinks and spare glasses to the table and set them down. The solidly built man did not shift his steady gaze from the doorway as he delved a hand inside a saddlebag, drew out a bill, checked the denomination and gave it to Regan.

"Cover it?"

"Change to come, stranger."

"Need more beer when the whiskey's gone. Let me know when the money's through."

All three raised the glasses of foaming beer and emptied them without pause.

"Do the honors, Stu," the eldest of the trio growled and the fat man uncorked the whiskey bottle and filled the shot glasses, while the medium in all things man continued to survey Millicent. And Regan, back behind his counter, leaned across it and lowered his voice to hiss:

"Either you go to work, girl, or you're out on your ass. And maybe the kid'll want you like a cold in the head."

The erstwhile whore looked set to snarl an angry retort at Regan, but swallowed her initial feeling about the threat and chewed on her lower lip. Then her worry-filled eyes found the unresponsive ones of the half-breed.

Edge finished his beer and pursed his lips as he rose to his feet. He said, "Life's full of problems. Only death solves them all."

The obvious leader among the trio of men snapped his head around to look at Edge as he heard movement. He saw the impassive half-breed heading for the doorway and found nothing menacing in the way Edge ambled, left hand tugging at the lobe of his left ear. He returned his attention to the doorway as the cloud bank which had been building in the north got extensive enough to mask the sun and cast a dull shadow over Ventura.

The fat man was alternately sipping his whiskey and rasping a pudgy hand over his jaw. The third member of the trail-weary trio was staring at Millicent again while Regan spoke words of anger softly to her.

When he had drawn level with where the leader of the bunch sat, Edge was close enough to see out over the batwings and confirm he had been mistaken. There were four horses outside: three hitched to the rail and one held on a lead line tied to the saddlehorn of another. This was Crystal Dickens's black stallion.

Across the street, the train crew were starting to raise and fix the sidegates of the freight cars which were loaded with sacks of ore-bearing rock.

Vince Attinger was approaching the end of the street from the direction of the tent in which Crystal Dickens was suffering.

The horny man said, "I reckon you're available if you want to be."

"Damnit, all right!" Millicent snapped at Regan and came fast to her feet.

"Okay, Max?"

The leader looked sourly from the man to the whore and back again and growled, "If you're that desperate, Johnnie. You never did have any taste."

"Hell, I ain't gonna eat it," Johnnie countered eagerly and started to spread a broad and lustful grin across his bristled face.

Edge halted and half turned, arousing the suspicion of the solidly built Max seated within arm's reach of him. And as part of the same move, the half-breed drew his Colt, thumbed back the hammer and squeezed the trigger.

The range was no more than four feet and Johnnie took the bullet in the centre of his forehead as he got to his feet. He was dead in an instant when the lead penetrated his brain. And there was just a small spurt of blood from the wound. Much more dramatic was the way he was impelled backward by the impact of the bullet, knocking his chair over and then draping himself across it. Limbs and torso and head limp while his belly was arched upward by the seat of the overturned chair. His death mask was the look of lust, but there was no longer any sign of sexual desire bulging the crotch of his pants.

Max, like Johnnie, never made it fully to his feet. He heard the gunshot, smelled the acrid smoke of the firing and knew one of his partners was dead without needing to see the hole in his head. And was certain he could avenge the seemingly motiveless and callous killing. But the Colt in the hand of the tall, lean, coldly grinning man cocked again and had swung to aim at the obese

Stu. And Max had his own revolver clear of the holster, hammer clicked back.

But the big built Max took note only of the Colt. He had failed to see the half-breed's left hand as it moved from tugging at an ear lobe to delve into the long hair at the nape of the man's neck. To come clear, at the moment of the killing shot, fisted around the handle of the straight razor slid from the neck pouch. Then, in a blur of speed which Max took to be a punch, was directed at his face. Half risen and half turned, Max was unable to back away because of the table. But instinctively he threw his head back to avoid the fist. An action that totally exposed his heavily bristled neck and throat.

Edge half turned his left wrist and felt just a slight resistence as the blade of the razor cut into the tough skin of Max. Then experienced the wet warmth of gushing blood on his hand and wrist as the blade opened up a deep gash in the side of the man's throat—long enough to sever the jugular vein and the trachea.

The gun in Max's hand exploded a shot, but he was already fighting for life giving breath and the squeezing of the trigger was caused by a nervous spasm. The bullet smashed into the frame of the batwings and the recoil tore the revolver from the hand as it was brought up, fingers clawed, to clutch at the lips of the fatal wound.

Stu had hurled away his whiskey glass and made to go for his gun as soon as Edge shot Johnnie. But then he froze when the Colt in the half-breed's hand covered him. Now he could only stare in horror as Max began to crumple with both hands clasped to his throat and blood oozing between his filthy fingers. A moist moaning sound was vented through the compressed lips of the dying man. Then the mouth was forced wide to give exit to a great splash of bubbling crimson. And Max was a falling corpse, his weight crashing against the table to send glasses, the whiskey bottle and the saddlebags to the floor. Bills spilled out of the saddlebags and Max collapsed across them and the rest of the mess his death had caused.

The fat Stu began to tremble as his flesh crowded eyes shifted from the dead Max to the aimed gun in Edge's hand and then up to look at the merciless face of the half-breed. He swallowed hard and sweat beads began to stand out from his every pore. He began to bring up his arms, to show his hands with the palms forward and fingers splayed in a sign of surrender.

"What . . . what . . . what did we do?" he pleaded as tears began to run down his bulbous cheeks, mingling with the sweat. "You ain't the law, are you?"

"Only to myself, feller," the half-breed answered evenly. He leaned across the table to add softly, "Just that you three had a run in with a lady I know. But the way it turned out, it wasn't her that was cut up by what you did."

Realization showed through the tears in Stu's eyes. Then Edge exploded a bullet into the fat man's heart and his eyes became glazed by death. He was rigid for a moment on the chair, then flopped forward, face crashing into the table top and arms flopping loosely to his sides.

The batwings banged inward and Vince Attinger came to an abrupt halt on the threshold of the saloon, cocked Remington clutched in his right hand—swinging to search for a target.

"Remember what I told you about aiming a gun at me twice, kid," Edge muttered as he wiped the blade of the razor clean of blood on the brim of Stu's hat, replacing it in the neck pouch.

"Why, mister?" Vince asked huskily as he slid his revolver back in the holster.

"Your money," the half-breed answered and began to eject the spent shellcases from his Colt and slot fresh rounds into the chambers. "That's it all over the floor."

"You didn't have to slaughter them that way, you murderin' sonofabitch!" Pat Regan accused shrilly.

Edge turned just his head to glance at where the saloonkeeper and the girl were standing in front and behind the bar counter—both their faces deeply marked by the lines of horror which the explosion of wanton violence had etched.

"Personal business between them and me, feller," he said as he holstered the Colt. "And dead men tell no tales."

"Milly!" the Attinger youngster blurted, and started toward her. "Milly, are you all right?"

The whore nodded, apparently unable to speak in the state of shock that gripped her.

"She's fine," Edge said as he stepped up to the batwings and pushed through them on to the decaying stoop of Regan's Place, and growled, "A piece of tail they only got to talk about."

Chapter Eight

THE train crew watched Edge come out of Regan's Place: the engineer and fireman from the footplate of the locomotive and the brakeman from the platform of the caboose, while the depot manager stared at the half-breed from where he stood beside a lever that operated the switchgear between sidetracks. All of them were obviously burned up with curiosity about the shooting in the saloon, but none was encouraged to ask questions by the demeanor of the tall, lean man who stepped down off the stoop and moved slowly along the street.

A few drops of rain fell from the grey, threatening sky and left large, short lived stains on the dusty surface of the street.

The depot manager yelled something in an impatient tone and the volume and range of sounds from the locomotive abruptly rose and was extended. It moved away from the line of freight cars then, after the switchgear lever had been thrown, and it reversed on to a sidetrack.

A few more raindrops spattered to earth. More forcefully than before, as if the clouds wanted to test by degree the response there would be to the impending downpour.

Walking slowly along the street, Edge was briefly aware that he was being watched from all over the tent town. But then it was abruptly the leaden sky that attracted the attention of the miners. And more rain fell, to beat into their upturned faces.

Edge halted outside the tent in which Crystal Dickens was resting and looked back along the wet darkened street, to watch as the caboose was moved by means of the sidetrack from one end of the line of freight cars to the other. Then, with the depot manager hurrying from one set of switchgear to another, the locomotive changed ends again. Next, when the entire train was back on a single track, the locomotive, cars, and caboose were rolled noisily together and the couplings were connected. A valve was opened to blast out a departure whistle and the train pulled away from the depot to begin its return shuttle to Colorado Junction.

The rain fell harder, pressing the steam and smoke from the locomotive to the ground, which shook beneath Edge's feet as the train rattled past him, gathering speed with every yard. The slipstream tugged at his hat and he had to grip the brim to keep it from flying off. The caboose rolled by him and within moments was lost beyond the curtain of rain. A gust of wind whipped out of the north, carrying the stink of the locomotive, flapping tent canvas and threatening to snag the hat from Edge's head again.

He turned, stooped and entered the tent, fastening the entrance flap behind him.

Crystal Dickens said, "I heard shooting, didn't I?"

Edge took off his hat and ran a shirt sleeve over his wet face as he sat down on the rocker.

The woman lifted her head off the pillow to look at his expression and was suddenly filled with dread.

"Yeah, lady, you heard shooting."

She swallowed hard and tried to rid her sun-punished and ointment-smeared face of the look of fear. She failed and dropped her head back on the pillow. Then she took the additional precaution of turning her face to the side of the tent.

"Did you kill anyone I know?" she asked huskily.

"Their names were Max, Stu, and Johnnie."

She became rigid under the blankets as the spatter of raindrops on canvas was briefly masked by the whine of the wind.

"Figure it was Stu who was for shooting you," he went on after the sound of the wind diminished.

"The big one. Very fat."

Edge made no response. He leaned forward to dry his hands on a blanket, then took out the makings and began to roll a cigarette. By the time it was finished and he had lit it, the woman had composed herself sufficiently to risk looking at him again.

"They deserved to die, Edge," she said and there was hardly a quiver in her voice. "After what they did to me. If I had been there, I think I might have been able to kill them myself."

"When there's killing to be done, best not to think about it, lady," Edge answered. "Just do it." He looked down at his wet shirt and pants. "Way things are right now, you get to live and I could catch my death of cold."

Just for a moment she was ready to deny knowing what he was talking about. But when she became as impassive as he was and her voice was as lacking in emotion when she said:

"They told you about stealing the money, Edge."

"They had your horse and a saddlebag full of bills, lady. Those two things added up to you being a liar."

"And you stood out in the rain thinking about whether or not to kill me for that?"

He said nothing.

"I'm sorry," she murmured against the sounds of the wind-blown teeming rain, and left another pause which he did not fill. Then she put more force into her words. "But think of my position. I had a lot of money that I thought belonged to you and I brought it right out into the wilderness to find you. And suddenly I didn't have anything. Except you. And while I was out at that old man's place I got to knowing you didn't want me. It was just like I told you it was. I just lied about not taking the money. I'm not a thief by nature, Edge."

She turned her head on the pillow to gaze at him again, displaying the intensity of her emotions on her scarred and greasy face. "I proved that when I brought the money from New York to Irving, didn't I? But I figured I deserved something out of all that happened. So I took what I could find and I started for home. And all the way across the desert and into the hills I kept thinking of things to justify what I was doing. That crazy old man had done what he wanted with a lot of the money. His son wasn't going to live. And his

93

grandson was young and tough enough to get by. While I was looking for you, I saw a lot of women who were forced to do every kind of rotten thing to keep from starving out in country like this."

She raised a hand and began to chew on the fleshy part of a forefinger, using this act to keep from crying.

Edge finished his cigarette and dropped it to the ground, where it hissed out in a pool of water which had run off his boots. "I'm due for a finder's fee from the Attinger kid, lady," he told her. "You should be well enough to travel when the train comes back to town. I'll buy you a ticket."

She looked at him again, watching him get to his feet, and was still close to fresh tears while her eyes revealed the struggle for understanding that was taking place in her mind.

"Why?" she asked. "I'm the reason you had to kill three men and—"

"Four, lady."

"Four?" she repeated and fear gripped her again.

"Feller who happened to be drunk while I was mad with you. I needed to wake him up and he didn't like the way I did it."

"Oh, my dear God," she rasped.

"No sweat," Edge told her. "Dead people are no trouble. It's the living that bother me. Some of them. I'll check when the train's scheduled to come back to Ventura."

He stooped and went out into the rain, ignoring the woman who called his name.

The wind had died now, as if it had fought a vicious battle with the downpour and lost. So that the rain lanced directly down, creating, destroying, and then creating again myriad pockmarks in the muddy surface of the street.

Edge was not alone as he trudged southward between the tents and toward the only frame buildings in Ventura. Miners, with chins on their chests and shoulders hunched, were heading in the same direction. The half-breed moved at a slow pace and as pairs and groups hurried past him, he caught brief snatches of sour voiced conversations.

". . . just like this time last year . . ."

". . . friggin' weather . . ."

". . . wash us all out, Goddamnit . . ."

"Bet that crazy old coot down south . . ."

". . . least he'll be dry aboard that tub of his."

The half-breed heard the disjointed exchanges and registered what was being said, but he gave the disgruntled miners' talk no consideration. His mind was concerned with Crystal Dickens—how she had been, the way she was now and what she would be in the future. And how much blame for the woman's state of mind and physical condition rested upon him.

The more he thought about it, his responsibility loomed larger. And his mood darkened to match the afternoon-into-evening atmosphere which surrounded him.

Then he was outside the railroad depot and he stepped up on to the boarding and pushed open a door beside a lamplit window.

The bald-headed and rotund Crane, minus his uniform jacket and cap, looked up startled from where he sat at a table, and sprayed fragments of bread and cheese when he blurted:

"Please, mister, I don't want no trouble! If I said anythin' that riled you I'm sure sorry."

Edge closed the door on the rain and sighed.

"Need to know when the train is due back here, feller."

"Another week, mister," the depot manager said after gulping down the food left in his mouth. "Weekly service is all that's necessary now most of the lode been worked out."

"Can I buy a ticket here for New York City?"

"New York City?"

By frontier standards, the room, which was part of the man's living quarters, was comfortably furnished with several mismatched items: a table and chair, two easy chairs, a bookcase, a writing bureau, a fireplace on which some logs flamed, pieces of carpet on the floor, a scattering of ornaments and two brass based oil lamps. The man kept the place clean and he was warm and had been enjoying a simple but plentiful supper before the stranger intruded.

"You must have heard of it, feller," Edge said, conscious of making this intrusion into the neat and tidy home of an innocent man and aware of the fear his very presence aroused in Crane. He felt an impulse to set the man's mind at rest, but not knowing how—and then not caring at all.

Crane nodded. "Sure, sure I know about New York City. But I can't issue you a ticket to get there. Just here to Colorado Junction, mister. Dollar and a half. Then you have to transfer to the Denver passenger train. Different railroad, so different tickets."

"Obliged," Edge said and made to turn. He speeded the move and dropped a hand to drape his Colt when the door burst open.

But it was only Vince Attinger who had hit the door hard at the end of a sprint across the street, making fast time to try to keep from getting too

96

wet. But he was soaked through to the skin anyway because of the fierceness of the deluge that was teeming down on this part of Utah.

The youngster closed the door and vented a whistle through his teeth as he shook his head to scatter water from his hair.

"Couple of men said they saw you come in here," he explained, then took note of Crane and his surroundings. And he was abruptly as disconcerted as the depot manager. "Gee, I'm sorry, sir," he told the railroadman, his hands toying nervously with the saddlebags he carried. "I figured this was a waitin' room or somethin'."

"We don't need one of them on a freight line," Crane answered with a scowl, not so apprehensive now that the young, clean-cut and apologetic Attinger was present. Then he shrugged. "But if you gentlemen have private business to discuss, my office is two doors down to the left. You're welcome to use it."

Attinger delved a hand into one of the saddlebags and brought out a bulging paper sack. "Just want to give Mister Edge this," he told the railroadman. Then, in a lower tone to the half-breed as the sack changed hands, "Ten percent fair? That's fourteen hundred."

"No complaint, kid."

"And I'll take care of seein' the dead get buried."

"Go along with that, too."

Attinger nodded, then began to fiddle with the saddlebags again.

"Something else on your mind?" the half-breed asked.

The youngster stared down at his muddy boots, then abruptly raised his head to meet the level gaze of Edge. "Those three men had the money. You reckon that means gramps is dead?"

"I don't know if he's dead or alive," Edge replied truthfully.

Attinger was not satisfied with this, but the cold impassiveness of the tall, lean half-breed offered no encouragement to pursue the point. And after a moment or so the boy showed a weary grin and raised the saddlebags a few inches. "I appreciate what you did to get this back, mister."

Then he pulled open the door and went out into the downpour. And just before he closed it behind him, the single note sound of the hissing rain was interrupted by the shrill blast of a locomotive whistle from some distance to the north.

Crane, who had been trying to conceal his interest in the talk behind a mask of irritation, was abuprtly anxious.

"Did I hear what I think I did, mister?" he asked.

"Sure wasn't a coyote, feller."

Crane left his supper and hurriedly donned his uniform jacket and cap which had been on one of the easy chairs. "Must mean they ran into some kind of trouble," he muttered as he brushed past Edge, jerking open the door and going out, leaving it open.

"Know the feeling," the half-breed growled and moved to stand on the threshold as the whistle shrilled again.

For a full minute there was nothing to see or hear except the visibility-restricting rain and the noise of its falling. Then the clatter of the approaching train sounded. Crane appeared from a doorway and moved to the side of the track, holding aloft and swinging a lamp. A pinprick of light showed in the north and grew larger as it came nearer. Men from the saloon emerged from the rain which acted like a curtain hung along the middle of the street. Questions were yelled to Crane and he ignored them as he moved the warning lamp more vigorously. Then the noise of the train covered all other sounds. The caboose with a lamp hung from the roof of its platform rolled into shadowy sight. A bell rang and brakes squealed. Freight cars clanked together and a great gush of steam hissed from the locomotive. The train halted, jerked, and then halted again. The hiss of escaping steam diminished and for long moments it sounded like the relieved sigh of a living thing.

Charlie the brakeman appeared on the platform of the caboose as men gathered around, demanding an explanation for the return of the train.

"Bishop Cuttin' is like a river, Mister Crane!" Charlie yelled. "Water rushin' down the grade like none of us ever seen it before! Maybe we could've made it, but we decided against tryin'! No way of knowin' what the water done to the track! That much water runnin' that fast! It could've washed away the whole bed from one end of the cuttin' to the other!"

"That's right, Mister Crane!" the young fireman confirmed as he and the engineer joined the group. "Best to wait until the storm's over so we can check on what the water's done to the track!"

"You done the right thing to come back," the depot manager told the crew as he turned down the lamp wick to douse the light. "Come on inside and dry out. Get some hot coffee down you."

Edge stepped off the threshold, out into the rain, as Crane led the train crew toward the doorway. Four looks which were a mixture of scorn and nervousness were directed at the taciturn half-breed, then the door was firmly closed.

The paper sack holding the money began to disintegrate under the assault of the teeming rain and Edge unbuttoned his shirt and pushed it inside as he started along the side of the stalled train. Then, with shoulders hunched and head down, he stepped off the boarding, across the track ahead of the now quietly hissing locomotive and started through the sucking mud of the street. He was halfway to the tent where he had left the woman, when he halted and listened. He concentrated the gaze of his narrowed eyes toward the sounds which had captured his attention, and in a few moments he saw a horse and rider loom out of the curtain of rain.

"Howdy," the man with a slicker draping him from shoulders to ankles greeted as he reined in his mount. "Guess this has to be Ventura?"

"Got it in one, feller," Edge answered and had the impression of a tallish, slimly built man in his own close-to-forty age group.

"Territorial Marshal Roche. Don't guess three strangers passed through here lately? One big and fat, one just big and one not much more than a kid?"

"Named Max, Stu, and Johnnie?"

"That's damn right!" Roche came back, his demeanor and tone abruptly grim. "How long ago were they through?"

"What's left of them is still here, marshal," Edge told the lawman, and jerked a thumb over his shoulder. "Ask at the saloon."

"What's left of them? You mean Max Sawyer and his partners are dead?" He was happily incredulous. "Somebody killed the sonsofbitches?"

"You've got it."

Roche vented a short laugh. "Well, I'll be. Is the man who got them still around, mister? Because if he doesn't know it, I've got some good news for him. Those sonofabitches were worth five hundred bucks apiece. Dead or alive. And dead makes it one hell of a lot easier for me." He laughed again, throwing back his head to turn his face at the downpour. "To hell with the lousy weather. Suddenly this is one beautiful day, mister."

Edge touched the brim of his hat and moved around Roche to finish the walk to the tent of another dead man. And said lightly, "Been something of a rewarding one for me."

Chapter Nine

CRYSTAL Dickens was no longer on the cot. Instead she was slumped in the rocker and there was exhaustion as well as pain etched into the punished flesh of her face which she had cleaned of the white salve.

The candle lantern was lit and its flickering flame spread a dancing light throughout the tent, so that by turns, her red blotched and yellow blistered features were shadowed and illuminated.

"The train," she said croakily as Edge entered. "I heard it come back. And I thought I could make it to the depot. This is as far as I got."

"Chance a section of track is washed out," the half-breed told her. "No rush until the storm's over."

He began to roll his blankets.

"You're leaving?" she asked anxiously.

"We both are. Just as far as Regan's Place. To get a solid roof over our heads."

"I can't . . . you'll have to help me."

"No sweat."

He lashed his topcoat around the bedroll and then carried the bundle and his saddle outside. Then he came back inside, doused the candle and drew a cry of mixed surprise and pain when he picked her easily out of the chair and ducked to carry her through the entrance flap. The force of the rain beating against her face took her breath away. Then she cried out again when he moved her in his arms and draped her over his shoulder.

"Ain't dignified or comfortable I guess," he said as he half stooped to gather up his gear with his free hand. "But like I told you, we ain't going far."

"It seems I have no choice," she rasped as he started to plod along the muddy street. "My God, I feel so helpless."

"No trouble, lady. I had to go back for my gear."

"And I'm just so much extra baggage you collected while you were there!" she retorted.

"Like you said," he answered.

"Said what?"

"You're a helpless case."

"My God, Edge, this is no joking matter," she said earnestly and he felt her press her face into his sopping wet shirt at the back. Then there was the threat of renewed weeping in her voice when she went on, "I really did mess it up, didn't I? If only I'd known you were coming back and waited at that crazy old man's place!"

They were at the end of the street and he veered to the side and stepped up on to the stoop of the saloon as she groaned, "Damn, damn, damn!"

Inside the place there were about two dozen miners, seated at tables or standing at the bar counter. Vince Attinger and Millicent were at a corner table on their own, talking with their heads together and holding hands like young lovers. Marshal Roche and the brakeman and fireman off the train were at the table where earlier three men had died. Pat Regan, smiling the first smile Edge had seen on his normally morose looking face, was behind his bar constantly surveying his rush of customers for empty glasses in need of refilling.

And most of the other people in the smoke-layered and liquor-smelling saloon seemed to be in a happy frame of mind. This was shown on their faces and heard in the buzz of talk. But then the conversations were curtailed and expressions became frozen on every face which was swung toward the pushed open batwings to see the half-breed cross the threshold with the woman slung over his shoulder.

"Frig it, what now, stranger?" Regan growled.

"She ain't for the cemetery, feller," Edge answered. "Too weak to walk is all. Need a room for her to rest up in."

For a moment or so it was as if relief had a palpable presence in the saloon.

"Hey, that the young lady Max Sawyer and his buddies mistreated?" Roche called above several restarted conversations.

"Right, marshal," Edge confirmed as he headed for the gap in the bar counter to which Regan had waved a hand. "I'll see you about the money on them right after I've got her bedded down."

"I'm not a damn horse, Edge," she rasped as he carried her behind the counter, and kept her sun-scarred face pressed into his back.

"Lady, if you were, I'd have shot you," he answered.

"Room five," Regan growled, jerking a thumb through the archway as he started to draw a beer.

The stairs were dimly lit from a lamp on the landing. Edge carried his burden to the top with

104

the same ease that he had brought them through the rain. At the designated door, he set down his gear to free a hand and turn the knob. Enough lamplight crept into the room to show him the way to the double bed and he lowered Crystal on to it gently. Then he went to the doorway and dragged his gear over the threshold.

The woman remained in the position he had left her, breathing deeply and obviously suffering from the effects of the uncomfortable trek from the tent.

"You want me to light the lamp?" he asked after glancing around the scarcely furnished, stale smelling room.

"Thank you, no."

"You want me to help you get out of those wet clothes?"

"I can manage."

"When you're under the blankets, don't spread out too much. I'll be up again in awhile."

"I've no right to object to that."

"You've got the right, lady," he told her as he raised one of the pillows and pushed his finder's fee beneath it. "But unless you make your point before my head hits this, I won't be able to hear it."

She had turned to watch what he was doing and when the pillow was back in place again, asked, "What's that?"

"Fourteen hundred bucks. My pay for getting the money back for the Attinger kid."

"You're awfully trusting of someone you know to be a thief," she said as he went to the open doorway.

"You can't walk, let alone run."

She snorted. "I just want one thing from you,

105

Edge," she said bitterly as he began to close the door.

"Yeah?"

"For you to make sure that train out there doesn't leave unless I'm aboard it."

"In my time I've broken a lot of things: from cups to most of the Ten Commandments, lady. Never a promise, though."

He closed the door and moved along the landing and down the stairs. Below, the saloon was again filled with cheerful talk and his reappearance among the customers caused no interruption.

Marshal Roche, who was of an age and similar build to Edge and wore a bushy, drooping moustache, was waiting at the bar beside the gap. He was reading a sheet of paper and there was a pen and bottle of ink beside his almost empty beer glass on the counter top. His tanned, green eyed features were arranged in a mild scowl when he looked up from scanning the note he had just written.

"I ought to be real mad at you, Mister Edge," he rasped through very white teeth. "For not telling me it was you who took care of Sawyer and his buddies. Made me look a bit of a chump when I asked around in here about it and was told I'd just been talking to the man that did for them."

"Ain't the right kind of weather for long talks out on the street, marshal. And you wouldn't have taken my word without witnesses to back it."

Roche scowled for a second more, then shrugged and folded the paper. "Water under the bridge now. Buy you a drink?"

"Sleep is what I need."

The lawman nodded. "Yeah, know what you

mean. I've got a lot of that to catch up on after being on the trail of those three sonsofbitches for near four months. Here."

He gave the paper to Edge.

"What's this?"

"My authority for you to collect fifteen hundred dollars from the Arizona Trust Bank in Tucson. In the event I'm not in town when you get there."

He finished his beer and banged the glass on the counter top for a refill. After it had been drawn and paid for, he said, "You didn't expect me to be carrying the cash around with me?"

The half-breed completed reading the simply-worded letter and refolded it and slid it into a hip pocket. "Guess not. Obliged to you, marshal." He patted the pocket where the letter was stowed. "Good as money in the bank."

"Sure is. And old man Clayburn who owns the bank will be real happy to pay up. He lost his wife and his only daughter when Sawyer and the others started blasting. And all they got for the killings was two hundred and four bucks." He raised his glass. "Here's to you, mister. And it's no skin off my nose, you collecting the reward money. My job don't allow for me to get anything except my regular pay. In case it bothers you."

"It doesn't bother me," Edge told him and turned to go back behind the counter. But halted the move when something heavy was banged on a table and the sound drew every eye to the corner of the saloon where Vince Attinger and Millicent were seated.

The youngster had used the butt of his Remington to call for attention and now he slid the gun back in the holster as he rose to his feet and grinned around at the sea of faces turned toward him.

"Want everyone here to have a drink with me!" he announced. "In celebration! On account that Milly and me are gonna get married!"

The news was greeted with a burst of cheering, whistling, and hand clapping. During which Pat Regan scowled his displeasure at the prospect of losing one of the few attractions his place had boasted. But then, as the calls for drinks began to be yelled at him and he started a tab for Attinger, his demeanor improved.

"Ain't you gonna take a drink with the boy?" the busy bartender asked of Edge as the half-breed moved toward the archway.

"Another time, maybe."

The gun butt hit the table again and Attinger was wearing an even broader grin and his voice was high pitched with excitement as he hugged the waist of the girl with one arm and draped the other around the shoulders of a moon-faced, thick-set miner.

"Make that two drinks all around, Mister Regan!" he yelled. "Mister Grimes here has just told me he's an ordained minister of the cloth! So he can marry folks! And tomorrow he's gonna marry Milly and me! Everyone's invited to the weddin'!"

This time the response to what the kid said was loud enough to mask the constant noise of the rainstorm for several seconds. By that time Edge reached the head of the stairs, where the barrage of drops beating upon the roof of the building acted to mute the raucous sounds of celebration from below.

Inside room five, which was at the rear of the

place, just an occasional shouted word or burst of laughter intruded into the pitch darkness after the door was closed.

Edge sensed that Crystal Dickens was only feigning sleep but he said nothing while he slowly undressed, relishing the lack of wet fabric pressed to his flesh when he was naked.

Then, "What's happening down there?" the woman asked as he dragged his saddle across to the side of the bed.

"The Attinger kid and the whore are getting married tomorrow," he answered as he arranged the saddle so that the stock of the Winchester jutted upwards from the boot. "He's throwing a party."

"Some people have all the luck," she said miserably.

"You're invited, lady," he told her as he slid his damp body into the bed.

"You know what I mean," she countered and jerked her warm body away from his cold one. She hurried to establish that the move was an involuntary reaction. "You're freezing."

She eased toward him and pressed her leg, hip, and arm against him to transmit some of her body heat to his flesh. And trembled.

"It ain't nothing to get excited about, lady," he said flatly.

This time it was the anger of humiliation which triggered her move away from him. She rolled on to her side with a groan of pain, putting her back to the half-breed.

"Damn you!" she blurted. "You don't have a single drop of the milk of human kindness inside you!"

"I was weaned early, lady."

109

"A person makes one mistake and as far as you're concerned they don't deserve the slightest consideration ever again. You know what I'm beginning to wish, Edge? I wish you hadn't found me today. I wish I'd stayed tied to the railroad track and the train ended it all for me. What then, mister hard as hails Edge? What if you'd found me cut up in a dozen pieces and spread out under a train? What would you have thought then?"

"Wishful thinking ain't something I ever do," he muttered. "Not like sleeping."

She sucked in a long breath and then let it out in a sigh that caused her to shudder. "How can a man as mean as you sleep at nights?" she asked bitterly.

"On this particular night, lady," the half-breed growled, "it seems like it's going to be with great difficulty."

Chapter Ten

EDGE woke at dawn, nudged from sleep by the first grey light of day spreading into the room from the single window. The rain was still falling from out of a leaden sky, but without the force of the previous night.

As always, the half-breed came awake to instant awareness of his surroundings and possessing total recall of the events which had led to him being where he was.

Crystal Dickens continued to sleep peacefully, undisturbed by the creaking of the bed as he slid from it. She remained so while he dressed in his underwear, pants, and boots, then washed up and shaved before putting on the rest of his clothes. And she merely moved her head on the pillow and breathed a small sigh when he pulled up the blankets to cover the exposed mound of one of her breasts.

Out on the landing he could hear the snores of men sleeping soundly behind doors. And as he went down the stairs the stale odors of last night's liquor, tobacco smoke, and sweat drifted into his nostrils.

He found the kitchen and had to rake yesterday's ashes from the stove before he could build a fresh fire. Then he put on a pot of coffee to boil and went through into the saloon. There he opened up the double doors and fastened them against the wall to either side. He stood for a long time on the crumbling stoop, breathing in the fresh, clear, damp air of the morning through which the rain now fell as no more than a depressing drizzle. When he heard the bubbling coffee boiling out of the pot spout and hissing on the stove he returned to the kitchen to pour himself a cup. Then he carried it out on to the stoop to drink it.

The new day was fully born by that time, dawn having pushed the last remnants of night beyond the towering cliff that formed the western horizon. But still there was no sign that anyone else had stirred from his or her bed in the tents and two buildings that comprised the dying community of Ventura. And while Edge drank the coffee and then rolled and smoked a cigarette, his continued to be the only pair of eyes to survey the morass of mud that was the street and trail, the silent train, the low grey sky, and the gently falling rain.

Then he heard footfalls on the stairway. They receded into the kitchen and a few moments later Vince Attinger emerged from the archway and crossed the saloon to join the half-breed on the stoop. He was carrying a cup of coffee in both hands and his youthful face had the dissipated look of somebody in need of at least a whole potful of the stuff.

"Shit, do I feel lousy," he groaned.

"Guess you won't be alone in that when the rest of them wake up, kid," Edge said.

Attinger's hands shook as he raised the cup to his lips. He shuddered when the coffee hit his throat, looked for a moment as if he might vomit it back up, but then swallowed it and grinned.

"Wow, that's good." He nodded. "And it was a good night. Maybe even worth feelin' this bad."

"Where are the bodies?"

The youngster blinked. "Oh, yeah. Out back in the stable. I said I'd take care of them didn't I?"

"No sweat, kid, I'll do the burying. It's not the kind of chore somebody should do on his wedding day."

Attinger's unwashed, unshaven, and liquor-pallored face became spread with an expression of doubt. "You think it's wrong of me, Mister Edge? Gettin' married the day after I buried my Pa?"

"You care what people think?"

"I guess I shouldn't. Except for Milly."

"The way it should be." He emptied the dregs from his cup and handed it to the young man. "Take care of this for me. I'll get to the burying."

"Somethin' I'd like you to know, Mister Edge."

"Yeah?"

"About Milly. She didn't come out here to do . . . to do what she was doin'."

"She told me, kid."

"She was lookin' for her sister and brother-in-law. Did she tell you that? They left Chicago to set up home in the west but after awhile their letters stopped comin' to Milly. She came out to look for them, just like Pa and me set off to find Gramps. But her money didn't last beyond here. And she ran up a debt with Regan. Helped him with the chores at first, but that just paid her way and she wasn't gettin' no stake to leave with.

113

Which was when she started to . . . when she took up the line of business she did."

"Heard that whores make fine wives, kid," Edge said evenly.

This caused anger to flare in the boy's bloodshot, red-rimmed eyes. "Last night, after Milly said she'd marry me, I promised her I'd kill any man who called her a whore."

"I've been warned," the half-breed said with a nod as a door opened and closed in the facade of the railroad depot building on the other side of the silent train.

Then he stepped out from under the stoop awning, sinking ankle deep into the mud as he angled across the street toward the caboose end of the train—the direction in which the footfalls on the boarding were headed.

"You want somethin'?" the fireman asked truculently when he saw the half-breed beside the track behind the caboose. He looked as if he had taken his share of celebratory drinks the previous night.

"Anyone checked on the flooded section of the line yet, feller?"

"That's what I'm gonna do now, soon as I've got Mister Crane's horse saddled." He turned to go around the side of the depot building.

"Obliged," Edge called after him.

The fireman cursed and the half-breed felt a stir of cold anger in the pit of his belly. But he curbed it and swung around to recross the street as Attinger turned to go inside the saloon.

Out back in the stable he saddled one of the dead men's geldings and took the corpses from the stall where they had been dumped, to tie them to the back of the horse. The bodies were starting to

114

stiffen but had not yet begun to smell. He found a long handled spade and with this canted to his shoulder, he led the heavily burdened animal out of the stable and up the slight incline to the patch of muddy ground featured with crudely fashioned crosses.

He relieved the gelding of the corpses before he began to use the spade on the soft and yielding earth. By that time the constant drizzle had soaked his clothing as thoroughly as the downpour of the previous night. And then his pores began to ooze with sweat for it was hard work to dig the hole large enough to accommodate three bodies. And eventually it was perhaps twice as large as necessary—crafter-shaped because the sides kept collapsing and spilling the near liquid mud toward the center. But finally he had a large enough area four feet deep into which he could drag the corpses and arrange them side by side. And then it was a matter, requiring little effort, of merely spading the displaced mud back into the hole.

It took the best part of two hours to complete the burial and then he marked the three-man grave by thrusting the spade into the ground directly above where the corpses lay.

He was content with the outcome of the thoughts which had occupied his mind while he was engaged in the self-imposed chore—that if there was room in his life for a woman, Crystal Dickens was not the one. Vince Attinger was young. He was resilient enough and sufficiently lacking in firmly held and deep-rooted convictions to excuse what his bride had been. Maybe he could even forget it. But in the half-breed's mind, no matter what else he felt for her, Crystal Dickens would forever be a thief and a liar. And this knowledge was no foundation upon which to build a lasting relationship.

He added a stream of saliva to the sodden ground, then rolled and lit a cigarette before he swung up astride the gelding. Lasting relationship, hell! There never had been any chance of that. The cruel fate that ruled the man called Edge had steered his mind to the decision that was made while he buried the trio of men. And it was lucky for the woman this was so—unless she really did have the death wish she had spoken of in anger the previous night. She was lucky to have survived this long in the company of Edge: with just a few bruises, some aching limbs and a bad attack of sunburn as physical evidence of the experience.

The sooner she was aboard the train heading north, while he was riding back south, the better and the safer it would be for her. But how could he tell her that, in words she would allow herself to understand? After she had constantly refused to accept the much more potent signs of impending doom which had cast an ever present shadow over them from the first moment of their meeting?

Gunshots exploded. A fusillade of fast-triggered rifle fire jerked the half-breed out of his morose reverie. He took his cupped hands from his lower face and took up the reins of the horse. Immediately, the half-smoked cigarette disintegrated between his lips. He spat out the mess of tobacco and paper and snapped his head around to seek the cause of the gunfire.

But there was nothing to see. While he had been sitting astride the docile gelding, deep in thought and detached from his surroundings, the drizzle had built steadily in intensity. And now

116

the rain was needling down from an invisible sky in a deluge that matched the storm of the previous night. So the slitted blue eyes gazing out from under the hooded lids could see nothing that was more than ten feet away from them.

The gunfire ceased after perhaps ten shots had been exploded south of the two buildings which marked the end of Ventura's single street, on the open slope across which the trail from old man Attinger's shack and ark came.

There was no cover out there, except the teeming rain in which a man could hide but that would not stop wildly fired bullets. So Edge thudded his heels into the flanks of the gelding to send the animal plunging down the slippery slope, pumping hooves exploding great sprays of mud, and heading for the rear of Regan's Place.

Now that the burst of repeater rifle fire was over, the hiss of the teeming rain masked out every other sound except that of the horse galloping over sodden ground.

When the building loomed ahead, the half-breed reined the gelding to a rearing halt, swung from the saddle, and left the horse to find his own way into the stable.

Two more shots were fired and, as in the opening fusillade, there were no follow-up sounds of the bullets crashing into solid objects.

Edge drew his Colt as he ran along the side of Regan's Place, cursing himself as a fool. For having reached his decision while he buried the men, there was no valid reason for him to involve himself further with Ventura, anybody who was rained in there, and whatever troubled the town or the people. And now, having instinctively reacted to the burst of rifle fire, he took the time to

117

consider the nature of the shooting, and realized it was not aggressive. Somebody moving fast off the slope south of town and racing on to the street, had emptied a repeater rifle at the pouring sky.

He slowed and stepped from the side of the saloon up on to the stoop. He halted there with a sigh in time to see a flatbed wagon slide through a forty-five degree turn as the slightly built driver leaned far back across the seat, feet pressed to the running board and hands hauling on the reins. A familiar looking wagon and a man who was unmistakable from his shrivelled, ill-clad body, grey hair and beard and toothless mouth. This last gaping wide to vent a roar of joy as the wagon rocked to a halt and the man jumped up bare footed on the seat.

Then, "All right you unbelievers!" Telly Attinger yelled in his seventy-year-old, reedy voice. "I forgive you! You laughed in my face and called me crazy! Now it's happenin'! It's comin' true! Just like I said it would be! Just like the good Lord told me it would come! Come on! Come with me to the ark! Before the flood waters burst from the mountains to engulf the world and all its wickedness! I waited for you! But you wouldn't come! Come now, before it's too late! Hear me! I forgive you! Come with me and be saved! You are the chosen ones! The good Lord directed me to come to—"

He swung his head to left and right as he ranted, his voice penetrating the hiss of the rain to draw people from beyond the teeming curtain of the downpour.

On the street at the side of the slewed around wagon, a group of bedraggled miners had trudged into view. Behind it, having climbed over the cou-

118

plings of freight cars stood Crane, the engineer, and Charlie the brakeman off the train. On the stoop in front of the batwinged saloon doorway was Pat Regan, Marshal Roche, and Crystal Dickens.

All the men looked hungover, sour-faced and irritable: An ill-tempered audience for the religious fanatic, resenting the fervid old-timer who had brought them hurrying out into the torrential rain by sounding off with a rifle, only to shriek his madness at their rudely awakened, liquor-sodden brains.

"Don't Vincent!" another voice screamed. It was Milly, from inside the saloon.

The old man on the wagon seat continued to rave of his crazed belief that the end of the world was imminent. But his head was tilted back now, contorted face turned to the full force of the beating rain as he gave thanks to heaven for deliverance, totally detached from his surroundings.

For stretched seconds, before the young girl's shrill voice spoke, Edge had also been preoccupied as he gazed along the stoop at the slender bodied, temporarily disfigured Crystal Dickens, who had sensed his presence and looked toward him—an expression of remorse and deep melancholy on her scarred face.

Then the girl shouted, footfalls beat on the floor of the saloon, the batwings were flung open and Vince Attinger lunged outside. The kid's right arm was thrust forward, the hand fisted around the butt of his Remington.

Crystal, Regan, and Roche scuttled clear of the boy and shouted at him. But his enraged words rang out clearly over what they said and the maniacal oration of the old-timer.

119

"You killed my Pa, you crazy old man!"

He leapt down into the mud beyond the stoop and the revolver in his hand exploded a shot. The bullet cracked through the rain and the boy's grandfather took it in the left upper arm. The old man was cut off in mid-sentence and his slightly built frame was twisted into a half turn by the impact of the bullet.

He stared down at the blood oozing from the wound, to be immediately diluted by the rain, felt the pain and raised his eyes to stare at the gunman. Sanity returned and he recognized his grandson, obviously recalling the events which had triggered the murderous rage inside the boy. He began to weep as he extended both arms toward Vince, in a gesture that was of submission and a plea for understanding.

Vince took a step forward, but his booted feet slid in the sucking mud and he dropped to his knees. He gripped the Remington in both hands, used both thumbs to click back the hammer and took careful, silent aim at the old man.

Aristotle Attinger began to sway. And moved his feet to retain his balance on the wagon seat.

Milly pushed through the batwings and came to an abrupt halt, mouth open to vent another plea to the boy. But no sound emerged and she was as dumb struck by horror as everybody else who stared through the rain at this prelude to cold blooded murder. Save one.

Edge had not holstered his Colt so he needed simply to twist his wrist and thumb back the hammer and squeeze the trigger to fire a shot from the hip over a range of twenty-five feet. It was too long for most men—even men with average experience of firing a handgun.

120

The bullet drilled through the back of Vince Attinger's left hand to make a neat, red rimmed hole.
It impacted with the butt of the Remington, was
instantly deformed, and so tore a ragged exit
wound in the palm of the boy's hand.

He screamed and the revolver flew from his
grip as he half turned on his knees, pitched forward and rolled over on to his back, clutching at
his bloodied hand with his good one.

This as his grandfather lost his balance, took
one staggering step and toppled over the back of
the seat into the bed of the wagon.

Edge was suddenly the center of attention. Eyes
swept to look at him as he tilted the gun skyward,
half cocked the hammer and turned the cylinder
until the chamber containing the exploded shell
was in position to allow for ejection. The case
dropped to the stoop between his feet and he took
a fresh round from his gunbelt and reloaded the
Colt, which he then holstered.

"Thank you, mister!" Milly blurted as she
jerked forward, half fell off the stoop while looking at Edge and dropped to her knees beside
Vince. "Oh, thank you!"

She embraced the injured boy and hugged his
head to her breasts, beginning to speak fast and
low to him.

But he broke free and shoved her roughly away
as he struggled to his feet, his eyes blazing with
hatred for Edge.

"Damn you, mister!" he snarled. "He murdered
his own son! My Pa! He had it comin' to him!"

"Today you're going to get a wife, kid," the
half-breed answered evenly. "You've got some
time to think now. Use it to figure out what's the
most important—relatively."

121

proach at Venturia in the back of the wagon, and as he went up and to the brink of Shantytown

Chapter Eleven

THE railroadmen returned to the depot and the miners trudged back to their tents. Vince allowed his soon-to-be bride to help him into the saloon and up the stairs to her room. Crystal Dickens, Pat Regan, and Roche watched Edge angle across the street to the wagon, pick up the unconscious old-timer and bring him—slumped over a shoulder— into the shelter of the stoop awning. Then they moved out of the way to allow him access to the batwings and followed him inside, where he lowered his burden on to the nearest chair and turned to go outside again.

"What's the idea?" the owner of the place snapped. "Dumpin' that crazy old coot here to bleed all over my floor. What am I supposed to do?"

"Make sure the kid doesn't make another try at him, feller. Until I've taken care of the wagon team. He gave them a hard time getting to town."

It took about five minutes for Edge to drive the wagon around to the rear of the place, take the near-exhausted horses from the traces and put them in the stable. He left the empty Winchester with which the old-timer had announced his approach to Ventura in the back of the wagon. And as he walked around to the front of the saloon, he was aware that the rain had started to slacken.

Inside, the fat Regan and the tall, heavily moustached Roche were standing on the respective sides of the bar counter, drinking coffee. Crystal Dickens was stooped over the slumped form of old man Attinger, bathing the flesh wound in his arm with a piece of rag and steaming water.

"Still out, uh?" he asked.

"Perhaps forever," the woman answered. "Being shot this way could kill a man as old as he is."

"Mister, that was some fine shootin' you did at the kid," Roche said with pursed lips. "I don't reckon I've ever seen a niftier shot than that. Over that range."

"Don't they say practice makes perfect, feller?" Edge answered as he sat down across the table from Telly Attinger.

"Max Sawyer and his boys couldn't have stood a chance against you. Real easy money you made." He banged down his mug on the bartop. "Here, Mister Regan, lace that with some rye."

"I didn't know I was in line for the bonus," Edge answered. "So it came real easy."

"But you had good reason for killing them, Edge," Crystal said softly. "Same as you have for anything you do. I can't understand why you kept the boy from avenging his father's death, though."

"Was young myself once, lady," he told her evenly. "Before I had too much time to practice. Had to learn by my mistakes. Never did get to kill my grandfather on my wedding day. But if there'd been a chance of that happening, I think maybe I'd have been obliged to whoever kept me from doing it."

123

The old man groaned and shuddered as the woman looked long and hard at Edge. And after stretched seconds shook her head as she said, "Guess you must know why it's so hard for me to realize that it's you talking?"

The half-breed glanced toward the doorway, out to where the light of early morning was brightening as the rain became less incessant.

"Pretty soon this weather will break, lady," he said. "And before long you'll be heading out of here on the train."

"That's no answer," she complained.

"Long way home for you. You'll have plenty of time to think of one." The old man groaned again, and smacked his lips. Edge reached out a hand, grabbed a fistful of the grey hair and lifted his head up off the tabletop. He said to the crinkled face, "You're going to be fine, old-timer."

Crystal gasped, then scowled as she picked up the bowl of red tinted water and said, "I'll get some fresh and see if I can help upstairs."

The old man's watery eyes opened and closed several times. Then they stayed open and peered hard into the impassive face of the half-breed. Next, as in the moments after he was shot, vivid memories crowded into his mind and recognition took the glaze from his eyes. Strength returned to his muscles and he straightened on the chair when Edge let go of his hair. He turned his head one way and then the other, taking in his surroundings, Regan and Roche at the bar counter, and the woman going out of sight through the archway. He looked down at the wound in his arm and grimaced. Then he took a double take at the doorway and the flanking windows.

"The rain? What's happenin'?" His eyes pleaded with Edge to give him a reassuring answer.

"World's as dirty a place as it ever was, feller. But seems the man upstairs ain't ready to make a new start yet."

"Crazy as a coot!" Pat Regan growled.

Attinger's face expressed depthless misery before he rested both elbows on the table and covered his features with both hands. His scrawny body shook, but he made no sounds. Until he groaned, "The boy said I killed Augie."

"He didn't lie."

"He tried to steal from me. The money was still in the house, but he didn't know that. He was fixin' to take it."

"He figured you stole it from him and his boy," Edge said as he rolled a cigarette.

"No. I had to do what I did. I saw the vision and I had to follow the signs the good Lord gave me. Augie was a fool. Like all those others who wouldn't believe me. I killed him. But I couldn't be sure it was what the good Lord wanted me to do. So I made off into the hills. To pray. To ask Him for another sign. And He gave it. After a night and a day of prayer, He answered me. With the rain."

"Which didn't drown nobody, old man!" Regan snarled.

Attinger dropped his hands to the table and if the movement triggered pain from his wounded arm, he did not show it. For he was again in the grip of religious fervor that made him insensible to all but the thoughts in his crazed mind.

"But it will! After I got back to the ark there was a pause in the deluge! Just a short time ago!

While the good Lord tested the strength of my belief and offered the unbelievers another chance! And now he is doin' so again! Not to test me! But to give all of you time to come back with me! Before the new rains start! And be saved when the waters of the flood torrent across the face of the earth!"

"Shit, why didn't you let the kid finish the old bastard!" Regan snarled. "So we wouldn't have to listen to all this crazy crap." He glowered at the disconsolate Roche. "You're a friggin' lawman. Ain't there some law that says you gotta protect ordinary folks from guys that are outta their minds?"

"I'm just a lawman in Arizona Territory," the marshal answered. "Unless I'm issued with a special warrant."

Regan scowled at him, at Edge and Attinger, and then toward the doorway. He growled, "Look, you old fool! There ain't no rain no more. No time at all the sun'll be out and it'll be as hot as Hades around here. Come sundown it'll be like no drop of rain ever fell on this godforsaken piece of territory."

"No!" Attinger denied forcefully, and snapped his head around. Then he moaned like a man enduring unbearable agony when he had to crack his eyes against the sudden brightness of the morning light.

Edge lit his cigarette, got to his feet, and stepped out through the batwings as a horse came splashing along the muddy street, under a sky that was visible again—higher than the last time it could be seen, the greyness of the clouds several tones lighter.

"What does it look like out at the cuttin'?"

Crane called from the railroad depot as the fireman reined in his mount.

"The bed held up fine," the youngster answered breathlessly. "We oughta take it slow, just in case. But I reckon we can roll just as soon as we've built up a head of steam."

"Get to work, son," the depot manager instructed.

Edge stepped down off the stoop and trudged through the mud of the street. Behind him, an upper storey window of Regan's Place was banged open. And Vince Attinger called:

"Like for you to hold the train until after the weddin', sir! Ain't no one more anxious than Milly and me to get out of this place as fast as we can!"

Crane jerked a watch out of his vest pocket and flicked open the cover. "Sixty minutes is what you've got, son!" he yelled. "Train time will be ten o'clock."

"Mister Edge!" the kid added and the half-breed halted and looked up at the window to see Attinger flanked by Milly and Crystal. The youngster wore a sheepish expression, his wife was smiling happily, and Crystal's sun-punished face showed dejection.

"You want something, kid?"

Attinger held up his left hand to exhibit the fact that it was neatly bandaged. "I went crazy and I'm lucky this is all that happened to me. I want you to know . . . hell, I'm glad you stopped me from killin' him."

Milly clung to his right arm and blurted, "What he's tryin' to say, mister, is thanks!"

He nodded vigorously and began to laugh. She laughed too, and it did not require any effort now.

"No sweat," he told them as he turned to continue across the street, and murmured, "Call it a wedding present for the happy couple."

Charlie the brakeman had taken charge of the horse and was leading it out back to the stable behind the railroad depot, leaving the young fireman and the engineer to go to the locomotive and prepare it for rolling.

Crane stood on the threshold of his living quarters, smoking a pipe and relishing what was left of a cup of coffee.

"Goin' to be a real fine day soon as that cloud breaks up," the depot manager said, and squinted toward the brightening sky.

"Like to buy that one way ticket to Colorado Junction, feller."

Crane sighed and turned to set down his cup inside the room. "Ain't much for talkin' chitchat are you, mister?" he growled as he dug a pencil and a pad of tickets from an inside pocket of his uniform jacket.

"No," Edge answered, and had the dollar and a half ready to hand over when the ticket was made out and torn from the pad. He said, "Obliged," when the transaction was completed.

Then he went back around the rear of the train and angled across the street to Regan's Place. But he did not have to go inside, for Crystal came through the batwings as he was about to step up to the stoop. He dropped his saddle and bedroll on the rotting boarding. Then held out the paper sack containing his finder's fee.

"Took out only enough to pay Mister Regan for renting the room," she said, her voice as lack luster as her expression.

"Here's your train ticket," he responded and

stooped to open a saddlebag and put the money inside.

She shook her head and kept her hands down at her sides as he straightened up. "I guess you'll be able to get a refund."

"Why should I do that, lady?" His tone and expression had a matching coldness.

"You don't have to worry, Edge. I'm still going home. But not by train. As far as Colorado Junction anyway. Marshal Roche said it would be all right if I took one of the dead men's horses. You can have mine until you find—"

"Fine," Edge told her. "What about train fare and eating money from the junction to—"

"I'll manage." She became grimly tight lipped.

"If you say so."

She turned and strode along the stoop. But before she turned to go along the side of Regan's Place toward the stable, she paused at the corner to tell him, "Thanks for taking care of me when I was in need."

She didn't look at him as she said this and then could not control the first of her sobs until after she hurried out of earshot of the half-breed.

The batwings flapped open and Milly came through them, a brand of sorrowful anger in her eyes, twisting her mouthline.

"You don't even know why she's leavin', do you?" she said in a tone of accusation.

"She's going home," he answered and stepped up out of the mud on to the stoop. There he began to roll a cigarette.

"I mean leavin' early. Not on the train. It's because she can't stand to be here when Vince and me are married. And then have to ride with us in the same railroad car after we've been married."

She was set to continue in the same manner, but then looked long and hard into his narrow-eyed, impassive face as he struck a match on the stoop awning support and lit the cigarette and said wearily:

"Yeah, of course you know." She raised a small hand in front of his face and clicked the thumb and forefinger. "And you don't give that much for how she feels."

Hoofbeats in mud captured their attention and they both looked along the street where it ran alongside the railroad between the scattering of tents to watch Crystal Dickens riding at a trot away from them. She did not acknowledge whatever it was Vince Attinger said to her as he and the erstwhile minister named Grimes emerged from a tent on one of the claims. And both of them had to jump back to get clear of the mud spray when the woman demanded a gallop from her mount.

"She's the saddest person I think I've ever met, mister!" Milly rasped bitterly. Then, as the half-breed stooped and picked up his saddle and bedroll, "You're leavin' now?"

The cigarette continued to slant from a corner of his mouth when he growled, "Yeah. It seems there won't be anybody to cry at your wedding."

Chapter Twelve

EDGE moved slowly along the stoop of Regan's Place, through the mud at the side, and went into the stable at the rear where he saddled the black stallion and lashed his bedroll into place. Then he led the horse outside and hitched him to the rail adjacent to the entrance of the store section of Regan's. All the time he allowed his mind the freedom to consider a reaction to Crystal Dickens's decision. But his mind remained as blank as his expression.

The jangle of the bell on the door brought the hungover Pat Regan shuffling into the small and overcrowded store.

"Yeah?"

The half-breed gave his order for supplies for the trail and the bald-headed fat man filled it without enthusiasm, laboriously listed the prices, added the column of figures, and growled the total. Then, after he had pocketed the money and Edge was gathering up the purchases, Regan asked, "You ain't stayin for the weddin' then?"

"No, feller. My presence ain't needed."

The bell jangled as he opened the door.

And Marshal Roche waited for the sound to

stop before he demanded, "Drop the supplies and reach, killer."

The lawman was at the rear corner of Regan's Place, aiming a cocked Winchester from the right hip.

"Object to having a gun pointed at me, feller," the half-breed drawled evenly.

"No countin' to three or any of that crap, Edge," Roche said coldly. "Just tell you that if you ain't done what I ordered before I stop talkin' I'm gonna blast . . ." The half-breed allowed the packs and cans to fall around his feet and raised his hands to shoulder height. " . . . you to kingdom come. Wise man."

Edge heard footfalls behind him and glanced over his shoulder to see the suddenly nervous Pat Regan advancing on the store doorway.

"Careful of that razor you say he carries!" Roche warned.

The half-breed returned his attention to the lawman and felt Regan snatch the Frontier Colt from his holster. He did not hear the series of metallic clicks that would have signaled the hammer being cocked.

"You're under arrest," Roche said and came closer to Edge.

"You got one of those special warrants to show me, feller?"

Roche halted with the muzzle of the Winchester held rock steady ten feet away from Edge. "Don't need one. What's called a citizen's arrest."

"For what?" the half-breed asked and half turned, facing Roche and able to see the still nervous Regan just inside the store out of the corner of his eye.

"Murder of Gerald MacArthur."

Edge shifted his slit-eyed gaze to look directly and coldly at Regan now. And the man back stepped as if there was a physical pressure emanated by the slivers of ice blue beneath the hooded lids.

"What kind of deal did he offer you, feller?"

"I done my duty is all, stranger," the owner of the place responded, quickly and nervously. "Just wish I was young enough to have done what the marshal is. Gerry wasn't much, but he didn't deserve to get gunned down by a pro killer like you."

He kept backing off as he spoke, until he came to a halt up against the store counter. The impact startled him and he gasped.

"And that's what you are, I reckon," Roche said. "Heard secondhand how you sent Max Sawyer and his sidekicks to the promised land. But folks often build up them kind of stories. Saw with my own eyes how you shot the gun out of the kid's hand."

Edge glanced just briefly at the lawman while he was speaking. For the rest of the time he concentrated his gaze upon Regan, and when Roche was through, addressed the frightened fat man.

"How's it going to be, feller? After I'm dead, he'll write another letter and you'll take it to Tucson? Collect the reward and split it with him?"

"Ain't no one else gonna get killed!" Regan blurted. "The marshal's gonna take you prisoner and ride with you up to Colorado Junction on the train. There's a Utah Territorial Marshal's office there and he'll hand you over."

"That's if you come peacefully, Edge," Roche added menacingly, his forefinger caressing the trigger of the Winchester. "If you don't, you'll still get the train ride. Only you won't know anythin' about it. So best you lower those hands and put them behind your back. So Mister Regan can tie your hands."

The half-breed was tensely afraid without showing it—for he knew the lawman from Arizona intended to kill him. Roche had put in a lot of hard time tracking down the three men who robbed the bank in Tucson. And he had probably done so as a dutiful lawman honoring the trust placed in him. No doubt he had been relieved to learn his quarry were safely dead, so that he did not have to risk his own life in capturing them and escorting them on the long haul back to Arizona.

But the rainstorm had trapped him in Ventura and he had begun to brood about the injustice of abiding by the law; his line of thought colored by liquor and its aftereffects. It had been four months of hard riding on rough trails for a marshal's pay. And when the job was done, there was not even the satisfaction of knowing he had done it well. What he did know was that another man had unwittingly finished it for him—and in the process, put himself in line to collect a fifteen hundred dollar reward.

Thus he was in the right mood to listen to Pat Regan's bitter words about Edge. His mind was a fertile bed into which the seeds of an idea were planted: to kill Edge and make a deal with a third party to collect the reward money and share in it. And as part of the deal, the third party was required to assist in the capture—for Roche was obviously afraid of Edge's deadly skills—and would not have dared to brace the half-breed alone.

Edge lowered his hands and swung them behind his back. Slowly. Apparently relaxed, but with every muscle tensed to power himself into a counter move should Roche's finger tighten on the Winchester's trigger.

"He has to kill me, Regan," he drawled, hearing the fat man's tread on the floor of the store but watching the marshal closely enough to see beads of sweat squeeze from individual pores. "You're right and he's right. I'm a killer. And he ain't about to hand me over to some hick town lawman he doesn't know."

"Shut your mouth!" Roche snarled, and licked some sweat off his moustache.

"He'll be afraid I'll beat this lousy rap. Or maybe I'll bust out of whatever kind of gaolhouse they have at the other end of this railroad spur. And in either event I won't forget about this."

"I said to shut up!" the lawman spat. "Get his hands tied, Regan. He's tryin' to scare you and there ain't no reason for you to be scared." He took a step closer to Edge. "He's just confessed he's a killer. And if we have to blast him for resistin' arrest, we're within our rights!"

Regan was breathing hard and fast behind the half-breed. He was breathing through his nose, as if terror was constricting his throat. He made a choking sound to clear the blockage before he could say, "Don't do nothin' to get yourself shot, stranger. That ain't my style."

The hand he used to press Edge's wrists together was greasy with sweat. The amount of planning which had gone on was evidenced by the fact that Regan had a ready prepared length of rope with a loop and running knot in it. He slipped it up over Edge's fingers and the backs of his hands. And as Edge's glinting eyes met the glassy stare in those of the lawman, he knew he was only a fraction of time away from seeing the muzzle flash of the Winchester and feeling the impact of a bullet in his chest, left of center.

Roche knew the tall, lean, brown skinned man in front of the rifle would not allow himself to be gunned down without an attempt to escape. And an attempt to turn the tables would be sufficient justification—to himself and to Regan—for the fatal shot to be fired.

"You saved my life, mister!" Aristotle Attinger said in his reedy voice as he swung into view around the rear corner of the building. And he squeezed the trigger of the Winchester leveled at Roche's back.

The hammer fell forward and the firing pin stabbed into an empty breech.

Roche had begun to turn his head when the old-timer spoke the first word, but without altering the aim of his own rifle. Then, on his face, the birth of mortal terror was aborted and the first lines of a triumphant grin began to be cut from the corners of his mouth and eyes. He then heard the series of metallic clicks and recognized the sounds for what they were.

And he squeezed the trigger of his Winchester to a more dramatic effect. But not the one he had intended. For in the time it took for the message of his desire to be transmitted from his brain to his trigger finger, the positions of Edge and Regan on the threshold of the store had been reversed.

The half-breed went through the doorway, starting the move the instant Roche began to turn his head. And as the loop tightened around his wrists he made a jerking action with his torso and arms which had a whiplash effect on the spare length of rope. And the startled Pat Regan did not

136

release his grip on this rope until it was too late.

He yelled his alarm.

Old man Attinger cursed at the rifle he had forgotten was emptied when he made his fervid entry into town earlier.

A bullet cracked from the muzzle of Roche's Winchester and drilled through Regan's left temple and exited from his right, boring a lethal tunnel in his frontal lobes in the process. It caused a long red stain, littered with tiny bone fragments to be laid across the mud close to where the corpse fell.

Once Regan had released his hold on the end of the rope, Edge threw his arms apart and the encircling loop dropped away from his wrists. He did this as he ran, footfalls thudding on the floor of the store. And he was free of the bond in time to use his hands to steer his leap over the counter.

"You crazy old fool!" Roche shrieked, and blasted a shot into the doorway. "He's a murderer!"

Other voices were raised, demanding to know what was happening in the saloon section of the building and out on the street.

The lawman turned bad worked the action of the repeater and exploded another shot as he stepped across the threshold. Like the previous bullet, this one slammed into the front of the counter which he could see provided the only substantial cover in the store. Wood splinters flew and the acrid smell of burnt powder masked the odors of foodstuffs which had earlier permeated the atmosphere.

Roche advanced across the store, the floorboards creaking under his booted feet.

"No more killin'!" Telly Attinger yelled. "There's been too much fightin' and dyin'! That's why the good Lord is gonna drown the wicked world in a new deluge!"

"Beat it, old man!" the Arizona marshal snarled. "This is law business. And the law can't wait for the man upstairs to clean the world of this kinda scum."

He fired another shot and Edge vented a groan of pain.

Roche laughed and muttered; "Got the bastard."

Edge hooked both hands over the top of the counter and started to pull himself up.

"Take me in, mister!" the old-timer implored. "I'm the real bad killer! I stuck a knife in my own son! And before that I—"

Roche came to a halt, Winchester barrel elevating a little as the half-breed clawed himself high enough for his face to show between his hooked fingers.

Milly reached the doorway of the store and screamed as she got a double-handed grip on the old-timer and dragged him outside.

Roche grinned broadly.

The reason for his joy and the girl's horror was the sight of the half-breed's face and hands above the countertop. His forehead, right cheek, and the right side of his jaw were smeared with bright crimson—as well as the fingers of both his hands. And on the side of his face that was unmarked he showed an expression of depthless hatred for the man with the aimed rifle—which abruptly changed to dread of the time that follows death. This lasted just a moment before the glinting eye

138

that was open squeezed closed. And the half-breed lost his grip on the counter to sink from sight and thud to the floor behind it.

"I got him!" Roche roared in triumph. "I killed the gunslinger!"

The news curtailed the shouting from outside. And in the hard silence that gripped Ventura, a bright shaft of sunlight punched a hole in the clouds to bathe the whole town with yellow warmth. And the lawman lunged forward to see and gloat over his victim.

He was still carrying the Winchester in a double-handed grip, ready to explode a final shot should Edge be not quite dead. And it was around the wrist of Roche's right hand—fisted to the barrel—that the half-breed wrapped his crimson stained left hand and wrenched it downward.

"Just ain't your day, feller," Edge rasped against the high pitched wail of shock and fear that was vented by Roche.

This he said as the marshal was hauled up from the floor in front of the counter, across its top and headfirst down behind it. The rifle exploded a shot, but the bullet went wild to the side and buried itself in a sack of flour. By that time the half-breed had a hold of Roche's left wrist. Having half sat up to reach, then folded flat to the floor again, this motion added power to the wrenching action that brought the lawman from one side of the counter to the other.

Roche's head hit the floor and Edge rolled up on to his side, using a shoulder into the other man's chest to send him crashing out full length on his back through the arch and along the hall-way that connected the store with the saloon.

Roche shrieked his pain at the impact and then fought to regain the breath which had been knocked from his body.

Edge powered up on to one and then both knees. He tore the rifle from the hands of the shocked and numbed Roche. He straightened to almost his full height, with one booted foot on either side of the lawman's ribcage. While he accomplished this series of moves, he worked the lever action of the Winchester. And when they were completed the rifle had a shell in the breech and the muzzle was aimed at the area of Roche's throat where the man's Adam's apple was frantically pumping.

The helpless man moved only those involuntary muscles that were keeping him alive. Thus, he breathed and his heart beat. For the rest he was absolutely still. Even his eyelids did not quiver and the pupils of his eyes where static as he stared his terror up the length of the rifle, the single hand that held it, the arm—and into the crimson-sheened face of the man he had been certain was dead.

The sun continued to shine, brighter and warmer by the moment. The fresh explosion of violent sounds inside the store had attracted other shouted questions from outside. But now the voices had dried up again and an even more tense and uneasy silence was insinuated through the town.

Roche worked his mouth and uttered nonsense. Then managed to choke out, "I thought I'd . . ."

Edge used his free hand to wipe some of the crimson off his jaw and then with a whiplash action of his wrist spattered droplets down on to the lawman's face. Roche closed his eyes by reflex action and compressed his lips in horror. Some of the drops adhered to his moustache and after a moment his nostrils twitched.

"Like it ain't always gold that glistens, feller," Edge said evenly.

Roche tentatively eased his tongue out through his lips and touched its tip to his moustache. Then he craned his head around and moved his eyes to the extent of their sockets to see if he could confirm what he suspected. And misery became mixed in with the fear on his face when he saw the overturned and uncapped bottle under the counter.

He looked back up at the impassive face of Edge and blurted hoarsely, "Tomato ketchup?"

"Ain't much of a breakfast for a condemned man," the half-breed allowed.

Roche gaped his mouth wide—perhaps to scream his fear, to curse in rage or, to plead for mercy. But the rifle muzzle was moved and the trigger was squeezed before the lawman could make a sound. It exploded a bullet between the lips, drilling a hole through the underside of the tongue and into the roof of the mouth, killing the brain and therefore the whole being, before it smashed out through the skull and came to rest imbedded in the floor. The shocked nervous system caused the body to convulse. Then the remains of Roche were still.

"Something with a little more substance, feller," Edge said as he swung out of his straddle of the corpse and placed the rifle on the counter top. "But seems it went up the wrong way."

He went along the back of the counter and then out to the front of it, crossed to the doorway and stepped over the threshold into the sunlight where he stooped to pick up his Colt from the drying mud beside the body of Pat Regan. Then Milly said huskily:

"Mister Edge . . . I thought for sure he'd shot you dead."

She stood at the rear corner of the building, pale and shocked. But not trembling to the same frenetic extent as old man Attinger who she was embracing, pressing his bearded face to her breasts.

The half-breed glanced in through the doorway to where a group of men advanced along the hall from the saloon and halted to stare down at the corpse with the bullet shattered head. And he rubbed ketchup off his face with a shirt sleeve as he rose and answered, "So did he, lady," he answered evenly. "But I had a surprise in store for him."

Chapter Thirteen

MANY questions were asked and answered. All of them were concerned with the reason for the two new violent deaths in Ventura.

But Edge heard none of the talk which took place in the saloon of the dead Regan. He was back on the patch of sloping ground which served as the town cemetery. He dug a two man grave this time, while Telly Attinger overcame what had been bothering him by satisfying the curiosity of miners and railroadmen who had not been in a position to see and hear everything that happened in and out front of the store.

The half-breed sweated a great deal as he dug the hole, dragged the bodies into it, and then shovelled the earth on top of them. The well-risen sun was now completely clear of the clouds that had broken up, changed color from grey to fluffy white, and scattered far and wide across the blue of infinity—blazing down to dry the sodden ground and erupt moisture from pores at the least exertion.

Frequently while he worked, he shifted his glinting eyed gaze northward. But all that moved out there was the rising vapor of rain water turned to steam by the heat.

Closer at hand, man-made steam hissed more strongly from the locomotive and billowed skyward to be neutralized at roof level between Regan's Place and the railroad depot.

His second burial chore of the day completed, Edge swung up astride the stallion and rode down to the street, the saddlebags bulging against his legs with the supplies he had retrieved from where he had been forced to discard them in front of the store.

A voice sounded against the hiss of escaping steam as he rode along the side wall of Regan's Place. A man's voice, intoning rather than speaking, in the regular, uninterrupted cadence of one reading aloud from a book.

". . . through Jesus Christ our Lord, amen," the moon-faced, solidly built Grimes said as the half-breed rode around the corner of the building and reined his horse to a halt on the street.

Many voices joined in with the final word of the prayer.

Grimes snapped a book closed and grinned as he said, "Congratulations. The groom may kiss the bride."

The marriage had been conducted on the decaying stoop of Regan's Place: Grimes with his back to the batwing doors, facing the young couple. These three were shaded by the stoop awning. The miners, railroadmen, and Telly Attinger were grouped in a half circle on the street. All of them except the old-timer were wearing hats to keep the heat and glare of the sun off their heads and faces.

Vince embraced and kissed Milly and many of

144

the men hurled their hats in the air as they cheered. Others simply cheered. Then all save the railroadmen and old man Attinger surged forward.

Crane dug the watch from his vest pocket, flipped open the cover and yelled, "Train time! All aboard!"

Then he nodded to the crew and the brakeman headed for the caboose and the engineer and fireman started for the locomotive. Some of the miners paused to kiss the bride as others hurried straight into the saloon.

Telly Attinger made no move beyond tilting back his head to gaze disconsolately up the small and widely scattered patches of white cloud which were all that was left of the storm front that had covered this area of Utah for so long.

"Wait for us!" the new Mrs. Attinger called to Crane. "We just have to get our things!"

She and Vince scuttled in through the batwings.

Edge heeled his mount slowly forward and reined him in close to where the wizen, raggedly attired old man stood—searching for something that was no longer there with eyes more watery than usual.

"Could be you kept me from getting killed oldtimer," the half-breed said.

Attinger shifted his gaze to Edge and for a stretched second did not recognize him. "What's that you said to me, son?"

"Usually, I'd kill a man who stole my horse."

The old man's face above the untidy grey beard became more deeply lined than ever as he struggled to find meaning in the words of the man astride the horse.

"That was your's, son? It was just the first that

come to hand. He's in the corral out back of my place again. No harm come to him. I ain't knowingly harmed no livin' thing in my life."

"Obliged to you for trying. When Roche had me covered."

Attinger squinted up at Edge. "I don't reckon you're a good man. But from what I've seen and heard you done around here, you didn't deserve to get killed like Regan and that stranger was figurin' to do."

Crane shouted something and the engineer sounded the locomotive whistle. The lively talk and laughter of the wedding celebration inside the saloon was abruptly diminished by an angry outburst.

"Waitin' for your lady friend?" the old man asked.

"She was a lady I made, feller." He curled back his lips to display his teeth in a grin of bitterness that did not reach his narrowed eyes. "Friends I don't make."

Then he and Telly Attinger snapped their heads around to look at the front of Regan's Place: The batwings crashed open and bounced hard off the wall to either side. But Vince and Milly were on the stoop and clear of the doors before they flapped closed. Their only luggage was a pair of familiar saddlebags which the girl carried draped over a forearm. Vince had his Remington drawn and cocked, leveled at his grandfather. Rage contorted his face. While his new wife expressed a desperate plea for help, her wide eyes switching back and forth between the youngster at her side and the stoic man astride the gelding.

"Don't you mess in this time, Edge!" the younger Attinger snarled.

"Best you take care where you aim that gun, kid," the half-breed responded flatly, and revealed no outward sign of the sudden tension that had built up inside of him.

"Why, boy?" the old man asked dully as inquisitive faces appeared above the batwings and the four railroadmen peered intently at the scene from the other side of the street. "You said you'd let bygones be—"

"The money!" Vince snarled and stepped down off the stoop, his boots cracking the sun-dried crust on the mud. "You used your share to build that crazy boat in the desert! Why the hell—"

"I was told to by the good Lord in the vision!" the youngster's grandfather countered.

"All right, you crazy old fool!" Vince allowed shrilly as he continued to close the gap between himself and the old man. "But that's done already! Why'd you take the other money? What d'you want it for? Where is it?"

"Money?" The old-timer was confused and tore his gaze away from Vince to look at Edge, Milly, the miners in the saloon, and over his shoulder at the crew on the locomotive footplate.

"Vince, it don't matter!" the girl cried and shook the saddlebags. "There's enough left here to give us a good start!"

"I ain't taken no money!" Tears spilled from the old man's eyes as he blurted the denial and backed away from the youngster bearing down on him. "Honest to the good Lord, I ain't never touched none of—"

His back came up against the side of a freight car and as he was jerked to a halt the words dried up in his throat. His grandson took two more steps and stopped with the muzzle of the Remington pressed to the flat belly of the old man.

The elder Attinger tilted his head back to stare at the sky.

Vince said tautly, "Ten thousand dollars! Where is it?"

Only Edge looked away from the two men beside the railroad freight car to peer for a stretched second along the north trail. But, of course, Crystal Dickens was far out of sight beyond the shimmering mist and the rugged hill country it hid—riding for home with precisely the same amount of money she had brought out to the west. But she had genuinely believed the first ten grand belonged to . . .

Edge swung his head to look back at the Attinger grandfather and grandson and was on the point of speaking up to save the old-timer's life, but the man had decided to be in command of his own fate.

He had looked at the sky for longer than Edge surveyed the trail. And the few flat bottomed white clouds he saw were as devoid of the threat of rain as the mist uncompromisingly veiled the long gone Crystal Dickens. There had seemed to be Divine intervention in the life of Attinger—while there had certainly been a worldly influence over the half-breed of late.

The shrunken old man did not have what it took to face up to his failure.

"All right, boy!" he snarled at Vince. "You wanna know the truth? Yeah, I took that money! I would've took it all if I could've carried it! And I've hid it in a place you'll never find it! Took it and hid it so you won't be able to throw it away on that whore you just got wed to!"

148

"No, Vince!" Milly shrieked and powered down off the stoop.

The youngster thrust the Remington harder into the old man's belly, his fist clutched to the butt as white as his face had suddenly become.

"But you got no call to have money worries, boy!" Telly Attinger goaded further, the force of his words causing a spray of spittle to fly into Vince's face. "Anytime you get short, that whore only has to lay on her back and open her legs and—"

The kid had squeezed his eyes tight shut. Now he snapped them open, vented an animalistic roar and squeezed the trigger of the gun.

His grandfather was silenced and became rigid against the side of the freight car.

"No!" Milly screamed. And was brought to a sudden halt from her run when Edge heeled his horse into her path.

Vince cocked the hammer and fired a second shot: The report muffled because the muzzle was sunk into the wound made by the first bullet.

The old man fought his pain to smile, then died. His body became limp and Vince stepped back from the crumpling corpse. A choked sound of horror was vented from his throat as he jerked the blood-dripping muzzle of the Remington out of his grandfather's belly.

"Easy, lady," Edge rasped at the girl. "Something you should know. So it won't make sleeping nights so hard."

She was anxious to get around the horse and rider but something about his icy tone and the earnestness of his demeanor held her rooted to the spot, looking quizzically up at him.

"It was an accident," the half-breed told her.

"But the old man your husband just shot killed those folks of yours you came out here looking for."

The news stunned her and she swayed a little, as if she were about to faint.

"They're buried decent, out behind his shack," Edge augmented. "But I figure there's no point in going there to take a look. Not if you really do want to forget everything about your old life."

"Train time!" the depot manager yelled. "Get this thing rollin', you guys!"

The locomotive came to louder life in response to the engineer's movements of controls.

Milly Attinger continued to stare up at Edge's face for a moment more. Then she pumped her head in acknowledgment of what he had told her, lunged to the side, and ran toward Vince.

The train whistle shrilled and masked whatever the girl said to the kid. The drive wheels of the locomotive spun, gained traction, and the whole train jolted forward. Milly tugged at Vince's arm. Vince shot a puzzle glance at Edge, then holstered his gun and allowed himself to be pulled in the wake of his wife. Next he took charge of her, helping the brakeman to get her aboard the platform of the caboose before clambering on to the moving car himself.

Smoke and steam hung in the wake of the departing train. Then it was gone, with only the smell of it lingering.

Edge moved his horse over to the side of the track where the inert form of Aristotle Attinger lay, curled in a ball and covering the stain of spilled blood. He drew a five dollar bill from his saddlebag and let it fall through the unmoving air. It came to rest on the bony hip of the old man.

He gazed out from under his hooded lids at Crane on the depot boardwalk and then across the street to where the miners had emerged on to the stoop of Regan's Place.

"Dug enough holes for one day," he said evenly. "That's for whoever buries him."

"That all you got to say?" the uniformed Crane growled.

"What else is there, feller?"

"A whole lot, mister. If you wanted. But you ain't the talkin' kind, are you?"

Edge looked again across the street to where the group of miners stood silently out front of Regan's Place. And answered, "Not the only one it seems. Appears the art of conversation is as dead as he is. Yet it ain't happened yet."

"What ain't happened?" Crane asked sourly.

Edge heeled his horse forward and looked from the dead old-timer to the sun bright sky and said, "Telly vision."